Jack
AND THE
WARDROBE

Jack

AND THE
WARDROBE

NICOLA JEMPHREY

© Nicola Jemphrey 2008
Reprinted 2008

ISBN 978 1 84427 269 3

Scripture Union
207 209 Queensway, Bletchley, Milton Keynes, MK2 2EB, England
Email: info@scriptureunion.org.uk
Website: www.scriptureunion.org.uk

Scripture Union Australia
Locked Bag 2, Central Coast Business Centre, NSW 2252
Website: www.scriptureunion.org.au

Scripture Union USA
PO Box 987, Valley Forge, PA 19482
Website: www.scriptureunion.org

British Library Cataloguing in Publication Data.
A catalogue record of this book is available from the British Library.

Printed in India by Thomson Press India Ltd.

Cover design by Go Ballistic
Internal design and layout by Author and Publisher Services

Scripture Union is an international Christian charity working with churches in more than 130 countries, providing resources to bring the good news about Jesus Christ to children, young people and families and to encourage them to develop spiritually through the Bible and prayer.

As well as our network of volunteers, staff and associates who run holidays, church based events and school Christian groups, we produce a wide range of publications and support those who use our resources through training programmes.

For Mum and in memory of Dad

Chapter 1

It was just my luck that the day I walked into the wardrobe I didn't end up in Narnia. Instead I was left with a sore shoulder and a massive bump above my right eyebrow.

"I can't believe you just did that, Jack!" said Mrs Armstrong, the assistant who'd thrown me out of the library at closing time a few minutes earlier. She had finished locking up and came rushing towards me. "That sculpture's been there for years now and I don't think anyone's ever bumped into it before – not before pub closing time anyway!"

She made me sit down on the dining room chair that was also part of the sculpture. Connecting it and the wardrobe was the figure of a man dressed in old-fashioned clothes. Like the chair and the wardrobe, he was made out of brownish metal. No wonder I'd taken such a battering. I felt a right eejit sitting there in front of the library while Mrs Armstrong inspected my forehead and the rush-hour traffic crawled past us out of Belfast. For once I was glad it was still getting dark early. Hopefully no one would notice me.

I was quite surprised Mrs Armstrong was treating me so kindly. After school and during the holidays, me and my mates spent a lot of our time winding up the library assistants. It was hard to miss the look of dread in their eyes as a crowd of us burst through the door at four o'clock, dragging our school bags behind us.

"Now then you lot, what can we do for you today?" Mrs Armstrong would say. One of the others would force themselves to smile.

They already knew the answer. Why else would we all drop everything the minute the school bell rang, and race each other down the road to the library? To be the first to use the Internet computers, of course!

"Stop pushing and form a proper queue!" they'd end up shouting as we all tried to grab the same pen to write our names at the top of the sign-up sheet.

"It's not fair, Miss, I was here before her," someone would always moan. But at last, under threat of us all being chucked out, we usually shuffled ourselves into some sort of order. Today I hadn't been among the lucky ones who got to sit in front of the screens for the next half hour. In fact, it would be five o'clock before it was my turn, which meant I'd only get 20 minutes before the computers were shut down ten minutes before closing time. I hovered behind the row of screens with my mates, watching a curly-haired 8-year-old girl dressing some woman from *EastEnders* in different outfits, and thinking how unfair life was.

"Right everyone, you know there's only one person allowed at each computer!" Mrs Armstrong sounded like she needed her tea break. "Find a book and sit down quietly until it's your turn."

"But Miss, she's looking at naughty pictures, Miss!" I pointed to the screen where the *EastEnders* woman was back in her underwear. "You should throw her out, Miss, and let me on instead."

Mrs Armstrong came towards me. "Are you going to do as I say, Jack, or will I have to ask you to leave?"

"Can't leave, Miss. The teacher told us to come to the library and find some books for our project."

"Oh, really?" She'd heard this one before.

"It's true, Miss. We've got to write about the life of a famous author. Isn't that right?" I asked some of the others from my class.

"Yeah, Miss, the teacher said we had to stay in the library till we find out all we need," one of my mates agreed. "You can phone and ask him, if you like."

"Then what are you all doing hanging around the computers?" Mrs Armstrong sighed. "You can use the Internet to help you look up information when it's your turn, but in the meantime the biography and autobiography sections are over there." With a look of relief she spotted one of the other assistants coming back from his tea break and escaped for a few minutes' peace and quiet upstairs.

Actually the bit about the project was true, but none of us had thought of starting it yet – we'd the whole term to do it. My mates, Rick and Tommy, flipped out a few books from the section Mrs Armstrong had pointed to and pretended to read them; another boy, Steve, sat down with a Spot picture book, opening and closing the flaps. I was about to go up to the desk and ask if I could look at one of the comics that were kept behind it, when I noticed a poster on the wall between the children's and adult fiction sections:

THE UK'S FAVOURITE BOOKS!
The books you voted as the best of all time.

A few weeks ago, I'd been in our lounge watching *All in This Together*, the latest TV talent show where people had to ring in and vote for who they wanted to play the main parts in a big new stage version of *High School*

Musical, when my dad came in and slumped down on a chair.

"This country's gone vote crazy," he moaned, snapping out a can from the six-pack he'd just dumped on the coffee table. "Toss me the remote control, son." He flicked over to Channel 4, which was counting down *The Fifty Cheesiest Hits of the Seventies*, and buried his face in his hands. "Give me strength, what will they ask us to vote for next? Will it be *The Top Thirty Pizza Toppings* or *The Twenty Most Disgusting Things to do with your Old Chewing Gum?*"

I laughed, but couldn't help thinking that he himself could probably present a show about *The Top 100 Brands of Lager*. He chucked the first can on the floor and cracked open the second one before channel-hopping back to BBC2. "Hang on, this looks more like it."

For a few minutes we watched a scene from the first *Lord of the Rings* film, which we'd rented out on DVD a few years before. I hadn't been too keen on it – the first bit reminded me of *Tellytubby* land, and the rest seemed very dark, but Dad had enjoyed it and I'd liked just keeping him company. We never seemed to do anything together any more. The clip ended and a celebrity popped up to tell us why we should vote for the book. ("Heaven help us, there's no escape," Dad groaned.) Next up was yet another celebrity, getting all worked up about some old book called *Pride and Prejudice*. Dad grabbed the rest of his cans.

"Can't stand books about women in frilly dresses," he muttered as he left the room. "Sort of thing your mum used to read."

I got up and closed the door to shut out the sounds of him stumbling upstairs. Dad had always had a thing about Mum being better educated than he was. I switched back over to *All in This Together* and missed the end of *The*

UK's Favourite Books. After that Saturday I'd forgotten all about it, but when I saw the poster in the library, I was keen to find out which book had won.

Dad would've been pleased; it was *The Lord of the Rings*. I wondered how many of the people who'd voted for it had actually bothered to read the book, rather than just watch the films. My eyes wandered down the list. There were quite a few children's books on it and one of them was sitting on the shelf underneath the poster: *The Lion, the Witch and the Wardrobe* by CS Lewis. I'd heard of it; there'd been loads of stuff on TV about the film a while back, though I didn't get to see it. I picked up the book, wondering if it was any good. If it had made the top ten, it must be.

"Isn't that a bit young for you?" Steve jeered, looking up.

"You can talk!" I laughed back, sending *Spot* spinning across the table as I sat down beside him.

Up until a few months ago I'd really quite liked reading, and when I was younger, I'd spent a lot of my time writing stories with complicated plots.

"Jack has a great imagination," one school report had said. "He just needs to ensure his stories don't become too far-fetched!"

Mrs Armstrong and the others sometimes used to keep aside for me books they thought I'd like. In those days I didn't give them too much trouble and it didn't really bother me if my mates gave me stick for being a big swot. It was worth it, having the chance to duck out of the real world for a while. I'd had a request in for ages for the last *Harry Potter* book, but when it finally came, I only got halfway through it. The library just gives you three weeks to read a book before you have to hand it back and it goes on to the next person on the waiting list. You'd think they'd give you a bit longer for a *Harry Potter*. I mean, how is anyone supposed to read all those hundreds of pages in three weeks – especially when you've just started a new school and have loads of homework? Back then I still did all my homework. Anyway, I had to give it back without even finding out what happened to Harry. I meant to put my name down for it again, but it was around that time I stopped caring – about flippin' well most things.

It felt good to get into a story again and before I knew it, I'd read the first three chapters.

"Five o'clock, boys!" I half-heard Mrs Armstrong call in our direction, and out of the corner of my eye I saw Rick, Tommy and Steve bolting past me towards the computers.

"Don't you want your turn, Jack?" Mrs Armstrong asked. "You only have a short time left."

I shook my head, keeping my eyes glued to the page. Just a few minutes later, it seemed, Mrs Armstrong came over to the table. "Come on," she said, taking the book from my hand. "It's almost half past five. I'll just mark this out to you and you can take it home."

I looked up, surprised. My mates had all gone and, apart from the staff, I was the only person left in the library. Mrs Armstrong stamped the book and I thumbed through it until I found the place where I'd left off. Holding it in front of me, I walked out of the library and straight into the metal wardrobe. In other words, I came back to earth with a bump.

"You really should get some ice on this straight away," Mrs Armstrong said, frowning at the lump on my forehead. "Will there be someone at home to see to it?" Then very quickly, she added, "I've been wondering for a while – is everything OK at home, Jack? It's just that I couldn't help noticing how your behaviour's changed lately."

"Oh, no, things are great," I said brightly, getting up from the chair and seeing stars. And they weren't in the sky.

"Steady on!" She grabbed hold of my arm. "Give yourself a few minutes before you rush off. Maybe I should give you a lift home."

"I'll be OK." Already I was feeling better, but I could see she wasn't going to let me go just yet.

"It's funny, you bumped into the very wardrobe you were reading about – well of course, not funny exactly, but you know what I mean."

"No," I said, gawping. "You mean this is the same wardrobe that's in the book?"

"Well it's how Mr Wilson, the sculptor, imagined the one in the book," Mrs Armstrong explained. "The whole bronze sculpture is a memorial to CS Lewis and his writings. But surely you knew that?"

"I've never really looked at it properly." To tell the truth, I passed it so often I hardly noticed it. It was like the lamp post outside our front door, or the Red Hand of Ulster mural at the bottom of my granny's street. "Is that guy meant to be CS Lewis then?"

"It's Digory Kirke, the Professor in *The Lion, The Witch and the Wardrobe*, but he looks like CS Lewis did as a young man." Her face suddenly lit up. "I know, why don't you base your project on the life of CS Lewis – there is a project, isn't there?"

I nodded and she went on, "As well as you having had a personal encounter with the wardrobe, it would be so much more interesting to do a project on a local author."

"Local?" I asked, puzzled.

"Of course. CS Lewis was brought up in this very area. In fact he was born about half a mile away, where the Dundela Flats are now."

I must be really thick. Why else would there be a big bronze statue of him in the middle of a pavement in East Belfast?

"And another thing," Mrs Armstrong was really getting into the idea. "You've got something else in common. You're both called Jack."

Maybe it wasn't just me who was thick. "I don't see any J in his name," I said, pointing to the cover of the book.

"His real name was Clive," she told me, "Clive Staples Lewis. But he liked his friends to call him Jack."

If I had a poncey name like Clive, I'd want to change it too.

"Anyway," said Mrs Armstrong, "if you want me to help you look for some information about him, I'll be in the library tomorrow morning. Remember we close at one on Saturdays."

"OK," I said. I had nothing else planned, and if I had to do a project on a writer, I might as well choose someone who came from round our way.

"Well, hope to see you then. You seem to be all right now, but do go straight home." She still looked worried.

"I'll be fine," I said. "I'm having tea with my Aunt Kate."

This did the trick. Mrs Armstrong smiled with relief.

"Oh, that's all right then. I'm sure she'll keep an eye on you."

I smiled sweetly and slipped away, wondering what she would say if she knew the truth.

Chapter 2

Five minutes later, I flapped through the doors of McDonald's and slid into a seat opposite a pretty blonde-haired girl. I hadn't really been fibbing to Mrs Armstrong. I wasn't on a date with my girlfriend – I really was having tea with my aunt, though not the sort of aunt Mrs Armstrong was probably thinking of!

I'd better explain. My granny had my dad when she was 17. He was the first of nine brothers and sisters. I was born when my dad was 19, so when his mum became a granny she was only 36. Less than a year later, my granny had Kate. She's my dad's sister, so that makes her my aunt, even though I'm older than her. As well as Kate, who's nearly 11, I have another aunt and two uncles who are even younger – Dean who's 9 and the holy terrors, Julie and Grant, who are 7 and 6.

Though I love my granny to bits and she says she loves me just the same as her own kids, there were times when I was younger that I thought it might be nice to have the type of granny you read about in books. The kind that knits you jumpers and gives you home-made lemonade and chocolate cake, not one you have to keep visiting at the maternity hospital. Then after the babies stopped coming, my granny, (who I've always called Eileen, because when I was born she thought she was way too young to be called Granny) was too busy looking after everyone to have time to spoil me. This was before Billy, my grandpa, lost his job at the shipyard and Eileen had to start working full-time at Tesco, as well as cleaning people's houses, to make enough money to keep everyone. Billy got really depressed after he was laid off and now he spends most of his time in the front room watching TV, so Kate ends up doing a lot of babysitting while her mum's out at work. She's really nice and hardly complains at all, so I like to take her out for a treat now and then, when Dad remembers to give me my pocket money.

"Jack, what've you done to your head?" she gasped, her blue eyes widening.

I told her what had happened and straight away she went up to the counter to order our meals and ask for some ice. I think some day she'll make a very good nurse. The queue wasn't too long for a Friday night and she came back a few minutes later with a tray of food and a cardboard carton, full of the kind of crushed ice restaurants use to make your fizzy drinks look bigger than they really are.

"You hold this on your bump while I sort out the food," she ordered, unwrapping the burgers and getting straws and napkins. We ate our meal pretty well in silence. I found it hard enough to manage with one hand, without having to talk as well.

"I think I've done this long enough," I said at last, setting the carton down on the table. The arm I'd been holding it up with now ached as much as my forehead.

"I bet you'll have a right shiner tomorrow," Kate said. "It's already started to turn a lovely shade of purple." She leaned across the table and asked in a lower voice, "So, any news from Caroline this week?"

I shook my head. It had been over three months now since my mum had left and we hadn't heard anything from her, not even a note to say where she was living. We knew she'd gone to London to try to "sort herself out", but that was all.

Kate knows when I don't want to talk; she's very good that way. She also knows that if I do want to talk to anyone, it will be to her.

"So will Mike be in when you get home?" she asked, gathering up all the food packaging and piling it back onto the tray. Mike is her brother and my dad.

"He said he'll be back around ten," I said.

Kate frowned. "Do you want to come home with me for a while? Mum's working tonight and I've got to put the kids to bed."

"Um, no thanks." I knew what would happen if I went round. Anytime I try to help Kate get Grant and Julie upstairs, they end up saying, "You can't tell me what to do. I'm your uncle (or aunt)." Then they try to force me to give them horsey rides around the back room. I've tried telling them nephews don't normally give rides to their aunts and uncles, but they never listen. They don't see why they shouldn't have everything their own way.

We'd just stood up from the table when Julie and Grant burst through the doors.

"*There* you are!" Grant cried, flinging himself at Kate. "We've been looking for you everywhere. Mum says you've to come home now!"

Julie spotted me tipping our rubbish into the bin.

"Aw, it's not fair. You two got chips and we only had stew. I'm going to tell Mum!"

I bought them a bag of chips and a drink each just to keep them quiet and walked with them to the bottom of their street, which was just around the corner from

McDonald's. Grant and Julie ran off to tell their mum about the chips.

"I'd better go," said Kate. "Mum needs to be out by seven. Will you be OK?"

"Yeah, I feel fine now," I said. "I might call down tomorrow afternoon."

"Oh, sorry, I won't be in. I'm going bowling with Heartbeat." Heartbeat was the club she went to at the church across the road.

"Right then, I'll see you Sunday. Your mum's asked me and Dad to come for dinner."

"Good," called Kate, disappearing up the street. "And thanks again for the McDonald's!"

I crossed the road and set out on the ten-minute walk towards my own house, passing the church where Kate, Dean, Grant and Julie went to different clubs. A couple of years ago, I'd asked if I could go to Heartbeat with Kate on Saturday evenings, but my mum had said no. She didn't explain why, just went all tight-lipped and strange for a while – even stranger than usual, I mean. I knew we weren't religious, but I hadn't realised Mum felt that strongly about not going to church. Then Dad told me it was because it was the church her dad used to be the minister of. I'd never seen my grandparents on Mum's side. All I knew was that Mum had fallen out with them years ago, before I was born. I'd always thought it had been because they hadn't liked Mum marrying Dad – they didn't think he was good enough for her or something. But after Mum left, before he'd started drinking so much, Dad kept trying to work out where things had gone wrong and he told me what had really happened.

"I think your mum expected her parents to disapprove of me," he said. "We both nearly dropped dead with shock when they said they were fine about us getting married. If

I'd had a daughter, I wouldn't have wanted her to marry someone as wild as I was then."

"Like, how wild?" I asked.

"Let's just say I had quite a reputation." Dad gave a quick grin. "We'd met at the club her dad ran on Friday nights for older teenagers. I only went along with some mates to cause trouble, but one night I met your mum and suddenly found myself wanting to impress her. I think she only went out with me to shock her parents, to get their attention. Well, if they were shocked, they didn't show it – they were the sort of people who treated everybody as if they were, I dunno, kind of *special*. Only maybe they needed to show their daughter she was more special than everyone else. They wanted us to wait to get married, of course, until Caroline had finished her A levels and university. I was happy enough about this. It would give me time to get a decent job and save up some money for a house. But after her mum and dad took it so calmly, Caroline went a bit crazy. She made me agree to run away there and then and get married in Scotland. Then, when we got back home, she said she didn't want any more to do with them."

"But didn't they try to see her?" I asked.

"Oh yes. We'd had to move in with my family and for the first year they called at the door all the time, but your mum refused to talk to them. Then, after you were born and we'd moved into our own house, they used to write and send presents, but she sent them all back."

I'd always known my mum could act a bit weird but I would never have thought she could be like that.

"I tried talking to her," Dad went on. "I wanted her to get together with them to try and patch things up, but it made your mum so mad I had to stop. Soon afterwards, her dad retired. (He and her mum had been quite old when she was born – maybe that was part of the problem.) They moved away from here to live in the country."

"Do you think that was what made Mum so sad, falling out with them?" I asked.

"Oh, I dunno, Jack," Dad sighed. "I've spent these last 13 years trying to work out why she was unhappy. The thing with her parents was part of it, but I think it was mainly that she didn't really love me – not nearly as much as I loved her, anyway. Probably she only stuck around as long as she did because of you, and maybe because leaving would have been like admitting to her mum and dad she'd made a mistake."

"But that didn't stop her leaving in the end," I said, fighting the tears that were attacking the back of my eyes.

"No it did not, son," Dad agreed sadly. "It did not."

I walked slowly on up the road towards home. The houses on our street were nicer than the one Kate and her family lived in – semi-detached with small gardens at the front and back. Dad had worked hard to get qualified and he earned quite a bit of money as an electrician. We'd moved from our first house to this house about five years ago because he'd thought it would make Mum happier. It was summer, and when the weather was good, she was outside most of the day, reading and doing a bit of gardening. Then winter came and she'd taken to her bed again. That was where I remember her spending most of her time, reading – to herself or to me – and crying a lot.

When I was a kid, I'd found it really hard coming home from school, never knowing if Mum would be downstairs getting tea ready or up in bed. As I got older, Dad and I worked out some easy meals I could make myself, like microwave dinners or pizza. Sometimes I got really hacked off about having to sort out my own food when most of my mates were going home to a nice meal. But that evening, as I turned my key in the lock and stepped into the dark hall, I would've given anything for Mum to be up in her room, waiting for me to bring her a cup of tea and tell her about my day.

I flicked on the light, picked up the day's letters from the doormat (bills and junk mail – nothing from London, as usual) and went into the kitchen, hoping Mary Poppins would have paid a surprise visit. But it was just as Dad and I had left it that morning. A mucky butter knife lay on top of the crumbs on the breadboard, last night's dirty dishes were still in the sink and empty beer cans overflowed from the rubbish bin. I rinsed a glass, filled it with water and got out of there as fast as I could. We could sort out the mess in the morning. Leaving the hall light on for Dad, I went upstairs to my room. I took *The Lion, the Witch and the Wardrobe* out of my school bag and set it on my bedside table. Then, even though it was early, I changed into my T-shirt and boxers, pulled out a letter from under my pillow and got into bed. This was the letter Mum had slipped under my door the night she'd left. It was beginning to fall apart from being folded and unfolded so many times, but for about the hundredth time I took it from its envelope and read:

Dear Jack,

I'm writing this to try and make you understand that I have to go away for a while, but that it's got nothing to do with you. You're the best thing that's ever happened in my life, but I've made a real mess of things. I need to get away from here to try and sort out where I've gone wrong. You may not hear from me for a while, but when I get settled, I'll write and tell you where I am and I hope you'll write back. But I'll understand if you don't. Just remember that I'll always love you and be thinking about you.

All my love,
Mum.

The letter had been written at the end of September. It was now January and she *still* hadn't let me know where she was. At the beginning of last summer Mum had stunned us by announcing she'd got a job in an office in town. She'd left the house every morning all dressed up and seemed a lot happier and more sure of herself. Then, just as I thought we were turning into a normal family, she upped and left. She'd left Dad a note telling him a job had come up with a branch of the same firm in London and that she had to go. She didn't want him to contact her – she said she needed time to think things through. But I hadn't thought she meant as long as this.

Fed up with turning the whole thing over and over in my mind, I put the letter back under my pillow and picked up *The Lion, the Witch and the Wardrobe.* As I read through to the end, I slowly realised I'd heard the story before. It must have been one of the books Mum had read to me on winter evenings when I was snuggled up in bed beside her. As I put the book down, I noticed it was half past ten. I couldn't believe it! Dad had *promised* he'd be home half an hour ago.

I got out of bed, took my mobile from my blazer pocket and tried his number. His phone was switched off. I went to the loo, got back into bed and lay there with the light on, my heart and sore head thumping. Just after midnight the front door slammed and Dad crashed upstairs. Relieved, I called out, wanting to tell him about my accident, but he mustn't have heard me. I switched off the light and finally managed to fall asleep.

Chapter 3

I'm on a beach with my mum and dad. The sand scorches the soles of my feet as I race Dad up from the water. We flop down on our towels on either side of Mum, laughing. She smiles as she sets down her book, and her eyes are a sparkle of blue, just like the sea.

The alarm on my mobile detonated under my pillow, blasting me out of my dream. Sleepily, I reached for my shirt from the tangle of uniform on the floor beside the bed. I always dress under my duvet on cold winter mornings. I was halfway through doing up my buttons when I remembered it was Saturday. Why on earth had I wanted to wake up early on a dark Saturday morning in January? The events of yesterday suddenly came back to me and my hand flew to my forehead. The bump had gone down a good bit from last night, but when I dragged myself out of bed and looked in the mirror I saw that Kate had been right. The yellowy-purplish bruise stretched from my eyebrow up to the roots of my hair. I wasn't a pretty sight.

I remembered the reason I'd set my alarm was so I could get down to the library early, before my mates were up. Reading novels was one thing; they were used to me doing that. But it wouldn't do a lot for my street cred if they found out I was thinking about my project already. I shrugged off my shirt and got dressed in jeans and a hoody. I decided to skip breakfast as I couldn't face the kitchen. There was always the *chance* Dad would've tidied it up by the time I got home.

I hurried down the road towards the library, blowing on my hands to try to warm them up. I thought back to the dream I'd been having just before I woke – of the hot sun and a sea you could plunge into without freezing to death. I must have been remembering the only foreign holiday we'd been on, when I was 9. We'd flown to Majorca and for the first couple of days the weather had been perfect. After that it had rained non-stop for the rest of the week and we'd all been really down in the dumps, not just Mum.

This morning was cold – dull and grey, with a wind that cut you in two. I felt it had been winter for ever, a bit like in Narnia, the country through the wardrobe, in the book I'd just read. Before Aslan the great lion arrived, it was always winter and never Christmas. Christmas hadn't really happened in our house either this winter. Dad hadn't bothered to get the decorations down from the attic, so it was left to me to drag down the green plastic tree, cover it with some tinsel and the only string of lights that still worked. We hardly got any cards. With Mum gone people must have thought they couldn't wish us Happy Christmas. That was the time I'd missed Mum most because though she hated winter, she loved Christmas and would always have been up and about for a couple of weeks beforehand, decorating the house and wrapping presents.

A few days before Christmas, a parcel had arrived, addressed to me in Mum's writing. I ripped it open, hoping for a letter from Mum to say how we could contact her or, even better, telling us she'd be coming home for Christmas. But all there was inside the big brown envelope was a present wrapped in Christmas paper, with a gift tag which just said, "To Jack, Love Mum".

I had to open it there and then to check she hadn't slipped in a note along with the PlayStation game she'd sent me. So all I had to unwrap on Christmas morning was Dad's present to me. It was a really awesome present – a mobile phone with a camera and MP3 player, but he'd given me the money a few days before and asked me to buy it myself. I'd even ended up wrapping it myself, so when Dad handed me the box from under the Christmas tree, it was hard to feel excited. I could tell he wasn't too rapt by the Bryan Adams CD I'd bought him, but we both put on our pleased faces though we knew we weren't kidding each other.

We'd gone round to Kate's for Christmas dinner, but the house was so crowded and noisy with the younger kids fighting over their toys, that we'd got away as soon as we could. I guessed Dad felt as glad as I did that Christmas was nearly over and we didn't have to pretend any more.

The shutters were still down when I reached the library, so I thought I'd take a closer look at the CS Lewis sculpture I'd been stupid enough to walk into. On the back of the bronze wardrobe was the head of a lion in 3D – Aslan, of course. Underneath this, a lot of words stood out. When I started to read them, I realised they were actually a letter CS Lewis had written to someone called Ann, who must have asked him what the Narnia stories meant. I was a bit surprised by what he told her.

Seemingly, Aslan, being killed by the Witch in Edmund's place and coming alive again, was like Jesus dying on the cross for human beings and then rising from the dead. I hadn't realised *The Lion, the Witch and the Wardrobe* had another meaning, I just thought it was an

exciting story. It put me off a bit. Kate believed in God and
Jesus and all that stuff. She told me she was praying for
me and Dad, and for Mum to come home. A lot of good it
was doing. If God was real, then he couldn't care very
much about my family. I thought of me waiting and
waiting for the letter or phone call from Mum that never
came, and waiting up late last night for Dad to roll in
drunk, and started to feel very sorry for myself.

A rattle of metal shutters told me the library was about
to open. Mrs Armstrong would be in there, waiting for me
to arrive so we could look for books for my project. Maybe
she'd even picked out some stuff already. I stepped back
behind the sculpture, out of sight of the library windows.
I wasn't so sure any more I wanted to do a project on
someone who had to go and spoil a good story with
hidden meanings. OK, Mrs Armstrong was expecting me,
but I quite liked the thought of a grown-up waiting for *me*
and wondering where *I'd* got to for a change.

By the time the doors of the library finally opened, I'd
crossed the road and was heading up towards the
shopping centre, where I bought some Coke and crisps for
breakfast and spent the rest of the morning looking at
PlayStation games.

As I left the centre, I met my gran, aka Eileen, who'd
just knocked off her shift at Tesco.

"Jack, love, Kate told me about your head," she said,
setting down her load of grocery bags and peering at my
forehead. "How do you feel today?"

"Better," I said, but I was only talking about my bruise.

"Oh, that's good. We're eating about one tomorrow. Is
that OK with you and Mike?"

"Yeah, fine thanks. See you then." Normally I would
have offered to help her carry her shopping home, but
today I just couldn't be bothered. Anyway, a couple of

days ago Dad had talked about going for a drive down the coast in the afternoon.

When I reached our house, there was a light on in the front room. Good, Dad must be up. Hopefully he'd made a start on the kitchen. As I was about to put my key in the lock, Dad opened it from the inside.

"Jack, mate," he said, pulling on his coat. "Where've you been? I'm just on my way to meet Len and Brian down the pub. Len's playing in a darts match this afternoon."

"I thought we were going for a drive!" I threw open the kitchen door to reveal an even worse mess than the night before. "And you haven't done the flippin' dishes!"

"I know. I slept in. Just you leave the mess and I'll tidy it up when I get home." Dad was trying to edge out the front door.

"You always say that and you never do!" I yelled at him. "And why are you going back to the pub so soon? You came in two hours later than you said you'd be last night. You just can't keep away from it!"

Now it was Dad's turn to yell. "I'm not going to be preached at by my own son!" he shouted. "There's little enough makes me happy these days. And Len's counting on my support. I can't let him down."

"But what about me?" My voice died away as the door slammed behind him. What was the point? It looked as if I'd be looking after myself from now on. Mum was gone and I couldn't rely on Dad anymore. He hadn't even noticed my bruise.

Fed up, I stomped upstairs and began to pick dirty washing off the bedroom floors. I'd have to get my uniform washed and dried before Monday morning. I was just coming down with the laundry basket when the doorbell rang.

"Hello, Jack, dear, I thought maybe you and your dad could use this casserole."

It was Mrs King, our next door neighbour. She and my mum had been quite friendly since they'd spoken to one another over the garden fence the summer we'd moved in. Any time Mum went next door to visit her she'd always come back looking more cheerful, which had made me Mrs King's biggest fan.

"That's great, thanks," I said, still cradling the laundry basket under my right arm.

"I'll bring it into the kitchen for you. You've got your hands full there. And what's happened to your head? You haven't been fighting, have you?"

"No, I just bumped into something." I stood back and let Mrs King pass into the hall. At the door of the kitchen she stopped dead. There wasn't a single empty space to set the casserole dish on.

"Right," she said after a moment, putting it down on a chair she pulled out from the table, "you put the wash on and I'll get stuck into the dishes."

She rolled up her sleeves and I knew I couldn't stop her even if I wanted to. It took over an hour, but by the time we were finished, all the dishes were neatly stacked in a cupboard, and the floor and work surfaces were gleaming.

"Thanks, Mary Poppins," I whispered.

"What was that?" Mrs King asked, filling up the kettle.

"Nothing, just thanks very much," I mumbled.

"No problem. I'm often at a loose end since Harry died and I miss your mum coming in for a chat. Is there any news of her?"

I shook my head.

"Poor lad," she clucked. "You know, when she took that job at the start of the summer I thought it would be the making of her. I was always telling her she needed to get out and meet more people."

"I think it just showed her what she'd missed out on," I said, swallowing hard. "It doesn't say a lot for me and Dad, does it?"

"Now don't you talk like that!" she said, putting a hand on my shoulder. "She was always talking of how much she loved you and how proud she was of you. And she'll be in touch when the time is right, I'm sure of it. Now let's have a cup of tea. Have you had lunch yet?"

When I said I hadn't, she made me sit down at the table while she put together some sandwiches. By the time I'd finished them and drunk a mug of hot strong tea, I felt a lot better.

"You make sure you look after yourself," Mrs King warned, rinsing the cups and plates and getting ready to leave. "I don't want your dad to think I'm interfering, but I'll try to look in on you every once in a while."

"Thanks," I said, "for everything."

After she left, I pulled the washing out of the machine and hung it over the radiators. The whole house soon reeked of lavender, but at least it was a fresh, clean smell. As I'd nothing much else to do, I spent the rest of the afternoon catching up on homework. When I'd finished, I went back into the kitchen to put Mrs King's casserole in the oven. If Dad came in late, he could always heat up his plateful in the microwave. I didn't see why I should have to wait until he took it into his head to show up. I was just setting the oven to the right temperature when I heard a bang at the back door.

"Jack, son," Dad's voice called, "come and see what I've got here!"

I switched on the outside light and opened the door.
Dad was balancing himself on a bike his legs were much
too long for.

"It nearly killed me riding this up from Brian
Campbell's," he grinned, getting off and stretching his
lanky body. "His son's grown out of it and he was asking
if any of us wanted it. I got it for a good price. Get on and
see how it feels. I know your old one's too small."

"Thanks, Dad." I tried to keep the surprise out of my
voice as I took the bike from him. The saddle would need
to be lowered but apart from that it was fine. I'd needed a
new bike for ages and would've asked for one for
Christmas, only everyone else was getting mobiles. I
hoped he *had* got it for a good price. He couldn't have
been making much money recently. People kept phoning
up and having a go because he hadn't turned up to do
work for them.

"That's all right, son. Sorry for shouting at you earlier.
I know this whole thing's hard on you, too. We'll maybe
go for that drive next weekend. And, look, I picked up a
Chinese for our tea."

I left my new bike propped against the back wall and
rushed back into the kitchen. While Dad was unloading
containers of fried rice, sauce, and cans of lager and Coke
from his rucksack, I slipped Mrs King's casserole into the
freezer and switched off the oven. Dad had tried hard to
show he was sorry and I didn't want him to know we
didn't need the Chinese. Amazingly, he didn't seem to
notice the change in the kitchen, but he did help wash up
the dirty plates before settling in the living room for an
evening in front of the TV.

I watched a couple of comedy shows with him, and
when he dozed off, I carefully removed the can from his
hand and went out to the garage. After fiddling around

with a few different spanners, I managed to adjust the saddle on the bike. It was already fitted with lights so I rode it up and down the street a few times, glad to clear my mind in the fresh air. Dad hadn't stopped drinking, but at least he was home tonight and we weren't still fighting.

And it did feel good to have wheels again!

Jack and the Wardrobe

Chapter 4

I'd left Dad snoring on the living room sofa, but sometime during the night he must have dragged himself upstairs to bed.

"Wake up!" I said next day, tugging off his duvet. "It's nearly a quarter past twelve and Eileen's asked us round for lunch, remember?"

He groaned and half-opened his eyes. "Not so loud, son. I've got the mother of all headaches. You go on without me. I don't think I could stick an afternoon of Grant and Julie."

"Well if you don't come, they'll be jumping all over me," I pointed out. "Couldn't we just go for lunch and say we have to leave early?"

Dad hauled himself upright. "Look, Jack, if I go round there, Mum will expect me to sit and talk to Dad, and to be honest, I haven't the heart for it right now. The way Dad is now, reminds me too much of how your mum used to be."

I could see what he meant. I didn't want him to feel any worse and start drinking even more.

"All right, I'll go by myself," I said. "I'll bring you back some dinner."

"Don't worry, I'll sort myself out with something," Dad said, heading for the shower. "Thanks for understanding. I'll see you later."

There wasn't much point in me not understanding. Any time I didn't, we just ended up shouting at each other.

Kate was very impressed with my new wheels.

"Wow, and it isn't even your birthday or anything," she said, as I chained it to the railings outside the front of her house.

"You can have my old one," I told her. "It's still in pretty good nick."

"It'd be far too big for me, silly!" she laughed.

She was right. I was quite tall for my age and she was the smallest in her class. She took after Billy, her dad, who was short and stocky. My dad must have got his height from Eileen, who was a few inches taller than her husband and used to moan that she could never wear high heels. My mum was tall too, so I suppose it would've been surprising if I'd turned out titchy.

"OK, I'll keep it for you until you grow up," I promised Kate. "If you ever do."

"Ha, ha," she said, leading me into the hall. "I'm not the one who goes walking into statues. Hey, Mum, Jack's here. Mike's not coming."

Eileen had managed to persuade Billy to join us at the kitchen table. He hadn't done that for ages and during lunch you could tell the others weren't used to having him there. Even Grant and Julie sat quietly and hardly said a word. Eileen asked me about school but Billy couldn't seem to bring himself to join in the chat. He was totally different from the grandpa who'd taken me round the shipyard when I was younger, showing me where he worked and talking proudly about all the great ships that had been built there:

"See that monster of a slipway down below us, Jack? It had to be specially built for the launch of the Titanic."

It had always seemed strange to me that people in Belfast were so proud of a ship that was famous for sinking, but of course, I never said this to Billy.

"It's been good to see you, Jack," he now said slowly, pushing back his chair and passing the plateful of food he'd hardly touched to Eileen. "I'm glad your head's feeling better. I'm sorry but I have to go now. There's a programme I want to watch at two o'clock."

"I'll bring you in some apple tart and cream," Eileen called, as he made his way back to the front room.

"No thanks, I don't really feel like it. I'll maybe take a wee cup of tea when you're ready."

As soon as he'd closed the door behind him, Dean, Grant and Julie became their usual lively selves, fighting over who'd got the biggest portion of apple tart and trying to be the one to tell me the corniest joke. Only Eileen was quieter than usual. For the first time, I noticed lines tightening her forehead and that she'd a lot more white hairs than fair ones. She looked, not old exactly, but a bit more granny-like than ever before.

"Mum's cracking up about Dad," Kate told me later. Some friends from across the street had called for the younger kids and we were up in the room she shared with Julie. "At the start, just after he'd lost his job, she kept thinking he'd just snap out of it one day. But it's gone on for ages now and he won't see a doctor, like Mum says he should."

"I didn't think he'd even come in for lunch," I said.

"Well, we'd told him about your accident and we knew he was worried about you, just like he was when Caroline first went away. Only he can't seem to think of other people for too long before he starts feeling sorry for himself again."

"I know," I said. "Mum was like that sometimes. It makes you feel kind of helpless because you can't do anything about it."

"Well I pray about my dad," Kate said. "That's something I can do, as well as doing my best to cheer him up."

I stared at her. "What are you on about? Praying isn't *doing* anything. You've been praying for my family ever since Mum went away and nothing's happened apart from Dad's drinking getting worse and worse!"

Kate was quiet for so long I thought I'd hurt her feelings.

"I'm sorry…" I began, but she stopped me.

"I know it seems weird to you, but the reason I pray has something to do with the statue you bumped into on Friday – the poached egg man. I only remembered it was him when I got home."

"What poached egg man?" All this praying must have made Kate go soft in the head.

"CS Lewis. There was a talk about him in Heartbeat last year and it stuck with me, maybe because the bit about the poached egg made us all laugh. He used to say Jesus could only be one of three things: a raving loony like someone who says he's a poached egg, an out and out liar, or who he said he was – the Son of God. From what we read about him in the Bible, there's no way he could be either of the first two things, so he must be the Son of God. And if you believe that, then you have to believe God is real and can answer your prayers. I know I'm not clever like you, Jack, but it just makes sense to me."

What Kate said was just like in *The Lion, the Witch and the Wardrobe*. Peter and Susan go to the Professor and ask why Lucy keeps insisting there's a world on the other side of the wardrobe. He tells them there are three possibilities:

either she's mad, she's telling lies or what she says is the truth. And of course, it turns out Lucy *has* been telling the truth. But that was only a story.

Kate was still talking. "There's a verse in the Bible that says, 'Ask and you will receive, seek and you will find, knock and the door will be opened to you.' I know God wants me to go on praying for you all and for my dad, even though nothing seems to be happening yet."

What if Kate was right and there really was a God who could answer prayers? For the first time I thought I should maybe try praying myself. It couldn't do any harm. But better not to say anything to Kate in case it didn't work and I ended up looking stupid.

"Oh well, I'd better go home and see what Dad's up to," I said, pushing myself out of Kate's beanbag.

"But aren't you going to stay for tea?" she asked. "Angela and the kids are coming, and Debbie and Niall." Angela and Debbie are Kate's older sisters.

"Not today, thanks. I saw them all at Christmas. I'll just go and say cheerio to your mum. See you next weekend. Want to go to the pictures or something on Saturday afternoon?"

"Yeah, OK," Kate replied, following me downstairs. "Mum's working Sunday so I'll be free all day Saturday."

When I got home, there was no sign of Dad, so I shoved the container of food Eileen had sent him into the fridge and went upstairs to my room. I knelt down by the side of my bed and then got up again, feeling really stupid. I was starting to go off the whole idea. What was it Kate had said: "Ask and you will receive?" It all seemed far too easy, as if you just said what you wanted and hey presto! God gave it to you! But Kate hadn't had a magical answer to her prayers, though she'd been asking for ages, so what was the point in me even trying? Then again, there was nothing else I could do to bring Mum back, so why not give it a go?

I knelt down again, closed my eyes and realised I didn't know what to say. So I just started: "Please God, if you're there, make Mum get in touch soon and help Dad stop drinking and make Mum come home so we can be a happy family…" I was about to add "again", but then I remembered we'd never really been a happy family, so I ended with "Amen." I got off my knees and decided to say this prayer every night and morning. Anything was worth a try.

For most of the next week I held out on going to the library.

"What are you up to these days after school?" Rick asked on Friday morning. "Strong Arm's been asking for you. Says she's got some books and stuff for your project. You haven't started already, have you? Sure we've got weeks to do it. I always do mine the night before."

"Course I haven't," I said. "I've just had loads of other stuff on."

The truth was I was bored out of my skull. I hadn't been going to the library because I sort of liked the idea of Mrs Armstrong wondering where I was. I'd hoped to go for a few bike rides after school, but the weather had been rubbish. I was also starting to miss the library computers. Our one at home had been broken for months and Dad had never got anyone to look at it, so I hadn't been able to check my emails.

By Friday, I was starting to see I was the one missing out, not Mrs Armstrong – she had plenty of other people to help. I wondered if she'd thought of ordering me any more *Narnia* books. I hadn't liked the idea of the stories having another meaning but I still wanted to find out if

Lucy and the others went back to Narnia and how they got there.

So, on Saturday morning, with the sun shining for the first time in ages, I cycled down to the library and chained my bike to the bronze chair. CS Lewis, or Digory Kirke, or whoever he was, didn't seem to mind – he was still staring into the wardrobe. Inside, I sat down at one of the computers and glanced around to see if I could spot Mrs Armstrong, trying to make it seem as if I wasn't looking for anyone in particular.

"Oh, Jack, are you looking for Mrs Armstrong?" Mr Bond, one of the other assistants asked from behind the desk. Before I could deny it, he went on, "She's off today, but she's left a pile of stuff for you on the shelf here."

"I'll just check my emails first," I said, not wanting to appear too keen.

This took all of three minutes, and after I'd logged off the computer, I collected the pile Mrs Armstrong had left and took it over to a reading table. On top, there was a note:

"Hello, Jack, I hope you're feeling better. This is all the stuff I've been able to find so far to help you with your project. The two biographies were written for adults, but you might find some bits and pieces in them and there are some good photos. There's also a pack about Lewis's life, written for schoolchildren. I've requested all the other Narnia books for you, but the only one that's come in so far is The Magician's Nephew, which is really the first book in the series, although it was written after The Lion, the Witch and the Wardrobe. If you need anything else, let me know. Mrs A."

As well as the things Mrs Armstrong had listed, there was a large booklet with a map and photos of the sights in the area to do with CS Lewis. Some of them were very close to the library. I checked out the books at the desk, put all the stuff in the backpack I'd brought and went outside to unlock my bike.

The place where he was born seemed like a good place to start what the booklet called *The CS Lewis Trail*. I propped the booklet open against the handlebars and biked the short distance from the library to a small block of flats in Dundela Avenue. There was a blue plaque on the wall to say that CS Lewis had been born there in 1898 – not in the flats, but in a semi-detached house that used to stand on the site, which was one-half of Dundela Villas. The booklet showed a faded black and white picture of the two houses; there were a lot more trees around than there are now.

Next I rode back towards Parkgate Avenue where Grandfather Lewis had lived. It was a long winding street and the booklet didn't tell you exactly where the house was. I'd almost reached the end of the street and was giving up hope of ever finding it when I spotted the chimneys of a big house, set back from the road. Ty-Isa, the booklet said it was called, going on to explain that this was Welsh for "little house on its own". CS Lewis' grandfather had come across from Wales to Ireland and had ended up in Belfast. Well the house wasn't on its own now – the row of terraced houses in front of it meant you could hardly see it. Maybe I'd have more luck with his other grandfather's house. According to the booklet he was once the Rector of St Mark's Church and the old rectory was still in the church grounds.

I panted on up the hill and soon turned left onto Holywood Road. St Mark's was just a bit further up on the other side. It was the church whose tower you could see from the far side of Belfast. The gate leading to the church grounds wasn't locked, so I rode through it and came to a standstill at the old red brick house to the right of the church. From the desks and computers inside, it looked as if it was now used as offices or something. The booklet pointed out the brass knob on the front door, which would have been at young Jack Lewis's eye level when he came to visit his grandparents. I bent down to look at it and saw it was a lion's head. "Was this where Lewis had first got the idea for Aslan?" the writer of the booklet wondered.

The door of the church was locked, but in the wall facing the old rectory, with the help of a diagram, I was able to find the stained-glass window Jack and his elder brother, Warnie, gave to the church in memory of their parents. It was meant to be a picture of three saints, with a tower in the background like the tower of St Mark's, but you couldn't really see much from the outside. Jack was baptised in the church by his grandfather in 1899 and became a proper church member when he was 16, by going through something called "confirmation". When he did this, he didn't believe in God but just pretended he did to please his father. I wondered what age he was when he *did* start to believe in God and what made him change his mind.

I'd have liked to visit some of the other places on the map, but it was nearly lunchtime and I'd arranged to meet Kate outside the cinema just before two. I put the booklet in my backpack and cycled home.

The weather turned windy and very wet again next morning and it was Wednesday afternoon before I had a chance to get back to *The CS Lewis Trail*. I was out of school as soon as the bell rang. I hopped on my bike and rode up Circular Road. Little Lea was the house on the right, just before the junction with Cairnburn Road. I mounted the pavement and stared up the driveway. It looked like the picture in the booklet all right, but it definitely wasn't *little*. It was a huge red-brick house with masses of windows (the kind with small square panes), high chimneys and a roof divided into lots of peaks. The booklet said that the attics in the house had given CS Lewis the idea for the attic tunnels in *The Magician's Nephew*. I was halfway through this by now and could just imagine Digory and Polly exploring the twists and turns under the different bits of roof. I thought about leaving my bike propped up against the hedge and sneaking up the driveway to get a closer look, but then I noticed the warning on the gatepost: PRIVATE. There was a car parked at the side of the house and I didn't fancy someone coming out and asking if I didn't know how to read.

At that moment there was the loud shudder of an engine behind me. A bus pulled up on the pavement, nearly knocking me off my feet.

"Sorry, mate," the driver called, over the slow hiss of the doors opening. "I'm not really supposed to stop here, but they wanted to get a good look at the house."

He pointed upwards and for the first time I noticed it wasn't an ordinary bus, but an open-topped one. The top deck was full of people talking excitedly in different languages and accents.

"It's the CS Lewis Tour," the driver explained, "the bloke who made that movie about the witch and the wardrobe. He was born here or something."

"Hey look, John!" A woman with too-blonde hair and a twangy accent was pointing me out to the man beside her. "Isn't he just a typical Irish boy, with that cute freckled face? Hey honey, could I possibly take a photo of you in front of the house? It would just make the picture."

I looked at the bus driver, who just shrugged. The lady clattered down the stairs of the bus.

"Say Lewis," she ordered, holding the camera out in front of her.

Seeing no escape, I flattened my back against the hedge and gave my cheesiest grin.

"Perfect," she smiled, pressing the shutter several times. "Now, if you wouldn't mind, I'd like my husband to take one of the two of us, from a different angle. John!"

John vanished from the top of the bus and joined us on the pavement. His wife handed him the camera and he took some shots of the two of us with the left side of the house in the background. At last she took her arm off my shoulders. I was about to grab my bike and make a quick getaway when the whole busload of people poured out of the doors, begging to take my picture or have one taken with me. This went on for about ten minutes until the driver, looking in panic at his watch, shouted he couldn't wait any longer.

"Wouldn't it be nice to finish up with one of all of us," the first woman said, waving her arms around to try to explain to the people who didn't speak English. "Would you mind, driver? You'd need to stand across the road to get everybody in. Oh, and the bus as well, of course."

She handed her camera to the driver, who looked as if he wished he'd chosen a different job.

"All right, missus," he sighed, "but then we really *must* be going, or we won't have time to drive to Crawfordsburn before it gets dark."

He crossed to the opposite pavement and all the tourists crowded round me in front of the driveway. As soon as he clicked the shutter, everyone else started to dodge the traffic to give him *their* cameras and he was forced to take more pictures until a horn blared in the driveway behind us. It was the owner of the house, wanting out.

"All right you lot, back on the bus. Enough's enough."
The passengers at last did as they were told and the bus
driver, with a red face, crossed back over and went to say
sorry to the woman in the car.

I'd had more than enough and sped off down the road,
with my new friends shouting "so long" and "au revoir"
as I went.

Chapter 5

The first Tuesday in February, I was heading out to school when Mrs King's face suddenly popped up on the other side of the fence.

"Jack," she said in a voice so low I could hardly hear it. "Has your dad left for work yet?"

That was a joke. Dad was never usually even awake by the time I left for school. He'd taken to staying later and later at the pub at night and I'd given up waiting up for him. I think he still did some work in the afternoons and early evenings, but as I hardly ever saw him, I couldn't be sure.

"No," I replied. "He's still in bed."

Mrs King glanced at our upstairs front room to make sure the curtains were still closed. "Then would you have time to come inside for a moment? I've something to give you."

Another casserole, I thought, turning out of our gate and into hers. Wonder why it can't wait till later? And why all the whispering?

Mrs King closed her front door softly and showed me into the lounge, not the kitchen. It wasn't a casserole then.

"This arrived yesterday morning," Mrs King said in her normal voice, taking an envelope out of a bigger one on the sideboard. "I couldn't bring it over in case your dad was there. Your mum was quite clear she didn't want him to know she'd written to you."

With shaking hands, I took the envelope from her. Mum had sent a letter at last! When I'd got home yesterday afternoon, I'd checked the post like I always did, hoping there'd be something from her but psyching myself up to be disappointed as usual. I'd never expected her to send it to Mrs King's house instead of ours!

Mrs King left me alone in the lounge while I read the letter. In it, Mum explained why she hadn't sent it to our house. She was giving me her address so I could write back to her, but she didn't want Dad knowing where she lived in case he came over to London and tried to get her to come home. She said she was missing me a lot, but was still thinking things through and trying to work out what was best for all of us. She'd made some friends at work and had gone out with them to see a couple of shows. She asked me to write and let her know what I was doing, but said she wouldn't be able to reply. She didn't want Dad to get angry with Mrs King if he found out she was passing letters on to me in secret.

"Are you OK, Jack?" Mrs King asked, coming back into the room. When I nodded, she went on, "I'm so glad you've heard from her at last. At least now you'll be able to write back and tell her how you are. Well, I suppose you'd better dash, or you'll be late for school."

Being late didn't bother me, but I didn't want to sit around and discuss the letter with Mrs King. Stuffing it into my blazer pocket, I thanked her, picked up my bike from where I'd left it in our driveway and set off down the road.

Praying really was just like magic! I thought, as I pedalled into the cold wind towards school. I remembered what Kate had said about asking and receiving, seeking and finding, knocking and the door opening. Well, I hadn't had to wait too long until I'd received one of the things I'd asked for. With a bit of luck, God would soon answer my other prayers, about Mum coming home soon and Dad giving up drinking. I'd start praying three times a day, no, four times. I could go into the loos at break and lunchtime so no one would see what I was up to.

"Don't you want to play footie with us?" Rick asked, as I tried to slip away from my mates after we'd finished eating lunch in the canteen.

"Uh, no, sorry. Got something to do. See you in Maths," I felt kind of awkward making excuses, but getting Mum back was more important than keeping in with mates.

"What about after school, then?" The afternoons were getting brighter and we usually had a kick-around before going home.

"Sorry, can't." I'd decided to go straight to the library and write my letter to Mum. I didn't want Dad catching me doing it at home. Part of me wanted to let Dad know where Mum was living so he *would* go over and try to bring her back, but I knew if she wasn't ready to come home, it might only make things worse. Maybe if I wrote and told her about the drinking and how miserable Dad had been since she'd left, she herself would realise she needed to come back.

After school I bought some writing paper, envelopes and stamps in the shop across the road and took them to the library. The computers weren't as busy now that it was light enough to hang around outside for a bit longer. The only person I recognised was Tommy's older brother, Andy, sitting in front of an orange and white screen.

"Hey, Jack," he said, giving me five as I went past. "I'm trying to find a cheap flight to London next weekend to see Sheryl, the babe I met on holiday last year. Take my advice, mate, don't start going out with an English girl – it's costing me a fortune!"

Smiling to myself, I sat down at a table with my pencil case and paper. Tommy had told us all how sloppy Andy had got since he'd met this girl in the summer. We'd all had a good laugh about it.

It took me ages to write the letter to Mum, and I used up nearly half the pad of writing paper. Well, I hadn't seen her for over five months and I wanted her to know exactly how things were at home so she'd see that she needed to come back as soon as possible. Too bad she wouldn't be able to write back and tell me how she felt about what I'd said. Then my brain clicked into gear. There was bound to be a computer at the office where she worked. Why not send my email address? That way she could write to me and Dad wouldn't find out.

I added my address and a note to the bottom of the letter, sealed the envelope and stuck on a stamp, so it was ready to post on my way home. After all this effort, I felt a bit flat. What should I do now? I didn't feel like going back to an empty house just yet. I might as well stay here until the library closed and do a bit of work on my project.

Glancing over at the computers, I saw Andy getting up and leaving. There wasn't anyone waiting to take his place so I picked up my school bag and walked over to the empty seat. As I set down my file block beside the computer, I noticed a small blue card. The name MR ANDREW JOHNSTON stood out in silver capitals. I ran out into the street and called after Andy, "Hey you forgot your credit card!"

He swung round and ran back towards the library.

"Thanks, mate. I owe you. I wouldn't want to lose this!"

Back inside, I stuck my memory stick into the computer and started to type up the notes I'd made over the past couple of weeks.

Chapter 1 – CS Lewis' Early Life

Clive Staples Lewis (or Jack as he preferred to be called) was born on 29th November 1898 at Dundela Villas in East Belfast. His father, Albert, was a solicitor and his mother, Flora, a clever lady who had studied Mathematics at Queen's University, something that was quite unusual for a woman in those days. His brother, Warren (known as Warnie), was three and a half years older than Jack, but the two were good friends. One of Jack's grandfathers (Flora's father) was the Rector of St Mark's Church. His other grandfather (Albert's father) was Welsh and was one of the owners of a firm called McIlwaine and Lewis: Boiler Makers, Engineers, and Iron Ship Builders. He and his family went to St Mark's Church and that is how Albert and Flora met. At first Flora didn't want to marry Albert, but he kept on asking and in the end she agreed and they were very happy together.

In April 1905, the Lewis family moved to a bigger house called Little Lea. At first Jack loved living there, even when Warnie was away at boarding school in England. His mother taught him French and Latin and he had a governess for his other lessons. He also had lots of free time for reading, which was what he liked doing best. The house was full of books and he was allowed to read them all, even the grown-up ones. During the holidays, he and Warnie spent hours playing in one of the attics they called "The Little End Room". They made up stories about a land called Boxen, which was full of animals dressed as knights that Jack liked to draw, and the trains and steamships Warnie loved playing with. Flora's cousin, Lady Ewart, and her family lived nearby in a big house called Glenmachan. The Ewarts were always asking the boys to come for lunch or go on picnics, or, what was really exciting in those days, to ride in their motor car.

But when Jack was 9, everything changed. One night he was feeling sick and wondered why his mother didn't come when he called. Then his father came in and told him she had cancer. After she died, Albert was heartbroken and wasn't able to comfort Jack and Warnie. He still loved them but became quite hard to get on with. Two weeks after Flora died, Jack was also sent away to boarding school.

"Jack, the computers will be shutting down soon, so remember to save your work," Mrs Armstrong called from the desk.

I clicked on the SAVE button and then reread what I'd just typed on the screen. I hadn't got very far with my project. It had taken me ages to pick out bits from the books and leaflets Mrs Armstrong had given me, and from some of the websites I'd found, and to put what I'd learnt into my own words. Most of my mates did what the teacher told us not to and just cut and pasted stuff straight from the Internet. But I didn't want to do that. I couldn't be bothered with most of my other subjects any more but I'd started to get really into my CS Lewis project. Maybe it was because he was from the same area as me, though he was a lot posher. There were other things we had in common – we were both called Jack, we both had one grandfather who was a minister and another who'd worked in shipbuilding, we'd both lost our mums (though, thankfully, mine hadn't died) and we both had problems with our dads.

But as well as all this, there was something else, to do with the *Narnia* books, that I just couldn't get out of my head. It was what Mr Beaver said to Lucy in *The Lion, the Witch and the Wardrobe*, about Aslan not being safe, but good, as if good was better than safe. All I wanted was to have my mum back so I could feel safe again. I couldn't imagine anything better than safe, but CS Lewis must have believed there was something and I wanted to find out why. And today, after one of my prayers had been magically answered, I didn't feel quite as prickly about the idea of Aslan being Jesus in another form. It was time I read some of the other *Narnia* books. I asked Mrs Armstrong if any had come in for me.

"Not yet," she told me, checking the shelves behind her and taking down a different book, "but I requested this for you. It's a teen biography of CS Lewis. Oh, and I thought you might like to watch the film *Shadowlands*, about his unusual marriage, so I've put in a request for that too."

Over the next couple of weeks I got into the habit of going off to pray on my own at break and lunchtime, and cycling to the library straight after school to check if there had been an email from Mum. So far there hadn't, but then the miracle happened that stopped me from worrying too much about that. Dad started cleaning the house and doing some shopping! Not only that, but he began to come home every night before I went to bed and, even better, his breath didn't stink of beer when he gave me a goodnight hug. The magic had worked again! I'd asked God to make Dad stop drinking and now he had.

"Praying is better than football – you should all try it!" I wanted to tell my mates, when they sulked about me not wanting to hang around with them. But I didn't have the nerve. Kate was the only one I could talk to about it and she was really chuffed for me. I felt bad that my prayers had been answered and hers hadn't, but I couldn't help feeling she must be doing something wrong.

"How many times a day do you pray for your dad?" I asked her.

"I'm not sure that matters as much as whether I really mean it when I do," she answered, looking a bit confused.

I didn't want to upset her by going on about it. Instead, I added Grandpa Billy to my own prayer list, sure he'd soon be up and about telling us stories at Mum's "welcome home" party.

A few days later I arrived home from the library with a couple of ready meals I'd picked up at the mini market and was met by the delicious smell of roast chicken drifting down the hall. This was too good to be true. I hurried into the kitchen where Dad was sloshing olive oil over potatoes in a roasting tin and looking stressed out.

"Oh, Jack, I didn't hear you come in." He slid the tin into the oven and slammed the door shut. "I should have had these spuds in half an hour ago. The chicken's nearly done and so are the vegetables."

I looked at the table and saw it was set for three. I was just beginning to wonder if Mum had suddenly come back and we were about to hold her "welcome home" party there and then, when Dad coughed a couple of times and said,

"I suppose I should have told you this morning, son, but I thought if I did, you might not turn up. I've invited someone for dinner, a friend I'd really like you to meet. Her name's Susie and she's a nurse. I got to know her when I went round to see about rewiring her flat. I was a bit of a mess at the time, but we got talking and, well, she's helped me a lot."

I couldn't speak. My dad had invited a woman to dinner who wasn't my mum. My dad had a girlfriend! I was just about to run upstairs and lock my bedroom door when the doorbell rang.

"That'll be her now," Dad said. "Please stay and eat with us, Jack. I know it's hard for you, but I just couldn't go on the way I was."

So this Susie was the reason Dad had stopped drinking, and not my prayers. Or maybe God had answered my prayers, but certainly not in the way I'd meant him to! I was so mixed up about this that I missed my chance to nip out the back door and was still standing there when Dad brought Susie into the kitchen. She was very different from my mum – fair haired, like dad, instead of a brunette; smaller and quite a bit younger. She looked quite unsure of herself.

"Hi there, Jack," she smiled nervously as Dad introduced us. "Hope you don't mind me joining you two for tea."

Of course I minded, but there wasn't a lot I could do about it. I sat and pushed the food around on my plate, grunting in answer to the questions Susie asked me about school.

"Aren't you going to have any more?" Dad asked when he and Susie had finished eating.

"No, I don't feel too good." Actually this was true – the smell of the chicken and roast potatoes was beginning to turn my stomach, and my arms and legs felt all achy. It must be the shock, I thought.

"Well, how about some of the dessert Susie's made?"

Dad took away the dinner plates and set the strawberry pavlova Susie had brought on the table.

"No thanks, I really don't feel well. I think I'll go and lie down."

Dad sighed, thinking I was making excuses, but Susie got up at once and felt my forehead.

"I thought you looked flushed. He's burning up, Mike. You'd better get him up to bed."

Startled, Dad helped me up the stairs and into bed. A few minutes later Susie came in with a thermometer, some iced water and a couple of tablets.

"39 degrees! There'll be no school for you for the next few days," she said, putting down the thermometer and handing me the tablets and a glass of water. "Now take these and try to get some sleep."

I don't remember much about the next couple of days except that Dad must have kept coming home in between jobs to take my temperature and bring me drinks. I slept a lot and had horrible dreams about Susie and Dad getting married, and me being sent off to boarding school.

On the third day, I woke up feeling hungry and thought I'd go down and get some breakfast, but my legs felt so shaky I didn't get any further than the landing.

"Dad!" I yelled, hoping he was in.

The kitchen door opened and Susie appeared in the hallway below.

"Jack, you're awake!" she called up. "Your dad had a big job on today and asked me to look in on you. Get back into bed and I'll bring you some tea and toast."

I was too weak to argue, though I didn't like the thought of Susie alone downstairs in my mum's kitchen – not that Mum had spent much time in the kitchen, but still. A few minutes later Susie appeared with a tray, which she set across my knees on top of the duvet.

"You're looking much better, but I still think you should stay in bed for a couple of days. You've had a nasty dose of flu. When you've finished this, you can show me where you keep your spare duvet covers and sheets. You can have a wash in the bathroom while I change your bed."

It was lovely to sink back into a clean, fresh bed. Guiltily, I realised I was enjoying being looked after. It had been a long time since my bed had been changed. Because I had to do it myself, it didn't get done very often.

"I see you like the *Narnia* books," Susie said, noticing *The Magician's Nephew* on my bedside table, along with the teen biography I'd started to read before I got sick.

"I'm on a waiting list at the library for the rest of them," I told her.

"I've got the whole box set of them at home. I used to love them when I was a kid. I'll bring them over later if you like. It'll give you something to do while you're lying in bed."

Because she'd been so kind to me, I didn't feel I could say no.

Jack and the Wardrobe

Chapter 6

In the end I was off school for nearly two weeks. During that time I read the other five Narnia books and more of the teen biography of CS Lewis.

The first school he went to in England after his mum died sounded like something out of Charles Dickens, with a headmaster who beat his pupils and in the end was declared insane! After this school closed down, Jack spent half a term as a boarder at Campbell College, about a mile from Little Lea, and was allowed to come home on Sundays. He would have been happy enough to stay at Campbell, but then he got sick. By the time he was better, his dad had decided to send him to another prep school in England, close to Malvern College where Warnie was a pupil. It was at this school, when he was about thirteen, that he stopped believing in God. He'd started to learn about other religions and beliefs and didn't see why Christianity should be the only true one. He thought the world was a bit of a mess and, if God existed, he would stop things going wrong.

Too right, I thought. My world was in a mess too. As long as my prayers were being answered, I'd been sure God was real, but then Susie had popped up. OK, she was very kind and nice, but that only made things worse. With someone like her around, how would my mum and dad ever get back together? This was the thing I'd prayed for harder than anything else and God didn't seem to be listening, though I kept on asking and seeking and knocking. Was I doing it wrong? I didn't think I'd changed the way I prayed, but maybe I had forgotten to say the right words. Yet... my other prayers, about mum contacting me and dad stopping drinking, *did* seem to have been answered. Maybe I shouldn't give up praying just yet. Maybe I needed to pray harder, more often. Maybe if I changed the words I used... Susie seemed to be the main problem at the moment so I started to pray, as often as I could, that she and Dad would break up (but that Dad would stay off drink).

As well as all this reading and praying, I spent a lot of time writing letters to Mum. I wondered if I should tell her about Susie, but decided not to. OK, it might make her jealous and bring her rushing home to try to win Dad back, but more likely, if she knew Dad had found someone else, it would put her off coming back altogether. I was quite sure if she did come home, Dad would forget all about Susie. Hadn't he told me over and over how much he loved Mum and hadn't he been heartbroken when she'd left? No, the important thing was to get Mum to come back, so I wrote her letter after letter telling her how sick I'd been and how much we needed her at home. I wasn't well enough to leave the house to post these letters so I slipped them to Kate when she called in with her mum to see me one day.

"I don't have enough stamps, but here's money to buy some more," I told her while Eileen was in the kitchen getting tea ready.

"There're loads of them!" Kate gasped when she saw the stack of envelopes. "What on earth have you found to write about when you've been stuck in the house for so long? But no problemo, I'll post them for you." And she stashed them in her canvas shoulder bag before her mum could see them.

By now I was well enough to be downstairs most of the time and it was good to get back to playing games on my PlayStation. Dad was in most evenings and we watched a lot of TV together. One night it suddenly struck me that Susie hadn't been around for a few days, yet Dad was still in a pretty cheerful mood. Could my prayers have been answered? Maybe I'd got the praying formula right again! As the days went on without Dad mentioning Susie, I became more and more certain I had. I thought of asking Dad what had happened to Susie, just to be sure, but I didn't want him to think I was missing her or anything.

By the Friday of my second week off school I was feeling much better and was fed up lying around the house.

"Do you want to do something tomorrow?" I asked Kate on the phone after she'd got home from school.

She thought for a moment. "Could we do that bus tour? You know, the one where the tourists all took photos of you. It sounded fun and it might help you with your project."

"Well, OK, but I'm not posing for anyone this time. I'll call for you tomorrow around eleven."

Next morning, I left the house at ten o'clock as I wanted to stop at the library to check my emails. Dad was already up and about, whistling as he fixed a dripping tap in the kitchen. Spring had arrived while I'd been stuck in the house, and crocuses and mini-daffodils were smiling from pots and flowerbeds as I walked down the street. I felt very hopeful things were going to work out OK.

It was a bit disappointing when I got to the library and saw there'd been no emails from Mum in the past two weeks. She should have got my letters by now. Maybe she didn't have an email address at work or wasn't allowed to send personal messages. Then again, all my other prayers seemed to have been answered, so maybe she was busy packing up and planning to surprise us all by arriving home any day now.

"Good to see you again, Jack. Are you feeling better?" Mrs Armstrong said as I stood up from the computer. When I nodded, she went on, "A couple of *Narnia* books came in for you while you were sick and also the DVD I told you about."

I told her I didn't need the *Narnia* books any more, but slid the *Shadowlands* DVD into my coat pocket and set off down the road towards Kate's house.

We got a bus into the city centre, and found the place where the special tour buses started from. The Titanic bus was about to go, but it turned out the next CS Lewis tour wasn't until two o'clock, so we looked around the shops for a while and had some lunch. When we arrived back at a quarter to two, the open top of the CS Lewis tour bus was already half full. I saw that the driver was the same one who'd nearly knocked me down outside Little Lea and hoped he wouldn't recognise me.

"Ha, it's the cute little Irish boy. I'll have to tell everyone to get their cameras out," he grinned, as I tried to hand him money without looking him in the face. "Only joking, mate. Put your cash away and go on upstairs. You deserve a free trip after what you went through a few weeks back – and you don't need to pay for your girlfriend either. Only make sure you don't tell anyone or I'll lose my job."

I opened my mouth to set him straight about Kate not being my girlfriend, then shut it again. He was the sort of man who'd never believe she was my aunt. But it was nice of him not to charge us anything. We climbed the stairs and found seats halfway down the bus on the right hand side. There were little headphones you could set to hear the tour commentary in your own language, so I switched mine from German to English, made sure Kate was OK and settled back to enjoy the trip.

First, the bus took us around the city centre and we saw the building in Royal Avenue where CS Lewis's father, Albert, had worked as a solicitor, and the Linen Hall library which Albert, Jack and Warnie used to borrow books from. Heading out to the east of the city, we passed Kate's street and waved at Dean, who was kicking a football against the boarded up windows of an empty shop. He looked totally gobsmacked to see us on the top of a bus with headphones clamped to our ears! We went past the sculpture outside the library, Dundela Villas, Ty-Isa, and St Mark's Church.

As we approached Little Lea, the commentary told us the new housing development across the road used to be the site of a house called Bernagh, where Jack's best friend, Arthur Greeves had lived. He and Jack had written hundreds of letters to each other during the years Jack lived in England, and Arthur had kept most of Jack's. When Jack was 33, just after he'd come to believe in God again and accepted that Jesus was God's Son, he'd stayed for a couple of weeks at Bernagh while he wrote *The Pilgrim's Regress*, his first Christian book for adults. Knowing how long it had taken me to write the first part of my project, how could anyone write a whole book in two weeks?!

I started to wonder again about what made Jack come back to believing in God, but just then the bus suddenly speeded up. I realised the driver was steering up past Little Lea as quickly as possible, before the voice on the commentary had even finished telling us about it! There was a lot of muttering from the other passengers. Kate and I looked at each other and tried not to laugh. A few minutes later we came to a roundabout and glimpsed the red brick towers of Campbell College through tall trees. It was a really old building, set in enormous grounds – very different from my own ultra-modern-looking school. I know Mum had been keen for me to try to get into a grammar school like Campbell, and I probably could have, if I'd wanted to, but I hadn't liked the thought of going to a different school from my mates. Maybe if I'd done what Mum wanted, she'd have been prouder of me and decided to stay with us. I tried not to think about this as the bus swung onto the dual carriageway, heading for the coast.

The headphones played music until we finally reached the village of Crawfordsburn, where CS Lewis and his wife, Joy, had spent their honeymoon. This was quite a long time after their wedding as Joy had been ill with cancer when they got married and everyone expected her to die. They'd actually had two weddings – one in a registry office after Jack had offered to marry Joy to stop her and her two sons from being sent back to America, and the other at her hospital bedside when Jack realised he loved her and wanted to bring her home to die at his house in Oxford. Only she hadn't died then; she'd made an amazing recovery and lived for three and a half more years – the happiest years of Jack's life, the commentary said. It suggested we should watch the film *Shadowlands*, which was based on the story of Jack and Joy. I took the DVD from my pocket and showed it to Kate.

"I'd like to watch it with you, but when Joy dies, I'll probably cry," she warned.

I was glad we'd gone on the bus tour as, apart from the few minutes near Campbell College, it had taken my mind off my own problems for a while. It also made me keen to do more work on my project. I'd taken some photos on my mobile from the top of the bus and over the next week I downloaded these and printed them out in the library. Dad was still in good form and was home every day by tea time. Susie seemed to have completely dropped off the planet. We just needed Mum there to make things perfect and I was working on that, writing her a letter every day, as well as praying hard.

The next Saturday, Dad woke me around nine o'clock.

"It's a gorgeous day," he said. "How would you like to go to Newcastle for a picnic? I've rung Kate and she's keen to come with us."

It had been a long time since I'd gone anywhere in the car with Dad, apart from to the supermarket. I got dressed quickly and ran downstairs to grab some breakfast while Dad loaded up the boot. We picked up Kate and then, just as we'd started heading out on the road to Newcastle, Dad turned into a side street and pulled up outside an apartment block.

"Susie's coming too," he explained, jumping out of the car. "She just got back from holiday last night and I thought it would be nice for us all to spend the day together before she goes back to work."

I felt as if I'd been punched in the stomach. So Dad hadn't broken up with Susie – she'd just been on holiday.

"Oh no, didn't Mike tell you she was coming?" Kate whispered, seeing the look on my face.

"No, he didn't!" I muttered back as Susie got into the seat beside Dad. She was tanned and glowing. If she'd been anyone else, I'd have thought she looked very pretty.

"Great to see you up and about again, Jack," she said, twisting round, "and I'm glad to meet you, Kate. I didn't believe Mike at first when he said he had a 10-year-old sister!"

"11 next week!" Kate smiled back at Susie.

We turned back onto the main road. Susie wondered what had happened to the postcard she'd sent us on the second day of her holiday.

"Oh well, postcards often don't arrive until after you've got back home," she said. "My mum didn't get hers, either. She didn't sound too pleased about it when I phoned her last night!"

I wished we had got Susie's postcard. At least then I'd have known she was only on holiday. Still feeling numb, I spent most of the journey staring out the window, only speaking when one of the others asked me something. But it really was a beautiful day and as we got closer to Newcastle and caught sight of the Mourne Mountains, I couldn't help feeling excited. One of the booklets from the library said that CS Lewis once told his brother, Warnie, that the countryside around the Mournes – the mountains, the rounded hills, the loughs and the sea – had given him the idea for what Narnia should look like. On a day like this, if you looked up from the busy road to the snow-capped mountains standing out against the blue sky, you could nearly imagine Fledge, the flying horse from *The Magician's Nephew*, soaring over them.

Dad parked the car along the seafront in front of an amusement arcade. "How about a go on the dodgems?" he suggested. "I haven't been on them since I was a kid."

Kate and I had never tried dodgems but they looked fun, so she and I got into one car and Dad and Susie into another. After the first go we swapped seats so Kate and Susie were driving. They did what they were supposed to and tried to dodge the other cars, so for the third go Dad and I had to take over again and make sure we bumped into each other as much as possible.

We went down onto the beach for our picnic lunch and while we were eating, there was a beep from Susie's handbag.

"A text from my sister to see if I've got home safely," she told us, peering at her mobile. "Only problem is I don't know how to text back."

"It's easy. Here, I'll show you," I said, reaching for the phone. Fifteen minutes later Susie was punching the SEND button after keying in a reply to her sister.

"I think I've done it!" she exclaimed.

She was even more excited when her sister texted back.

"She got it!" Susie yelled, nearly dropping her mobile.

"Told you there was nothing to it," I said, as we all laughed.

After the picnic, we went for a walk along the beach.

"Susie's nice, I really like her," Kate said.

In front of us, Dad put his arm around Susie's shoulders and I was suddenly jerked back to reality. Somehow, without me realising it, the four of us had spent the day playing "happy families" and things had got way too cosy. Something would have to be done before Dad forgot all about Mum and decided he wanted to marry Susie instead.

Now I just had to figure out what.

Jack and the Wardrobe

Chapter 7

We got back to Belfast around teatime and Dad dropped Kate and me off at the chip shop around the corner from our house.

"Get yourselves a couple of fish suppers," he said, handing me a tenner. "I'm just going to take Susie out for a bite to eat, but I'll be back by nine to give Kate a lift home."

Kate and I sat in the kitchen and ate our tea without talking much. I was racking my brains thinking what I could do to bring Mum back and get rid of Susie.

"Well we can't sit around all night doing nothing," Kate said at last, carrying our plates over to the sink. "Could we maybe watch the *Shadowlands* DVD?"

At least this would keep Kate busy until Dad came back, and I could carry on trying to work out an action plan without feeling I had to talk to her. We went into the living room and I put on the film.

I'd been learning so much about CS Lewis over the past few weeks that I ended up being drawn into the story without meaning to. I thought Anthony Hopkins acted out the part of Jack really well, though apart from wearing the same kind of tweed jackets, he didn't look much like the photos I'd seen of him. For some reason the film made out that Joy only had one son, Douglas, instead of two. I suppose it made the story a bit simpler.

As I watched, it struck me that some awful things had happened to CS Lewis: his mum had died of cancer when he was very young and so did his wife a few years after they were married. This was all the sadder because he hadn't found someone he wanted to marry until he was nearly 60! On the bus tour we'd been told his dad had also died of cancer when Jack was still a young man. I wasn't surprised Jack started to doubt God near the end of the film. What *was* really amazing was that after writing a book about his grief for Joy, he kept on believing and trusting in God until he himself died a few years later. How could he *not* have stayed angry with God after all the bad things that had happened to him?

During the drive back from Newcastle all I could think of was how God had let me down. He seemed to answer my prayers at first, but now, with Dad and Susie closer than ever, he'd knocked me right back. I didn't see how anyone could have prayed harder than I had. No, praying wasn't the answer. I *had* to come up with a better idea to get Mum to come home.

Kate managed to get through the film with just a few sniffles.

"I wonder why they went to that place in England for their honeymoon instead of to Crawfordsburn like they really did?" she asked when it was over. "I know it was the place in the picture in Jack's study, but why couldn't the picture have been of Crawfordsburn instead? And how come Jack was driving Joy in a car? I thought it said on the bus tour he never learned to drive."

"No, he was never much good at practical things because his upper thumb joints didn't bend. That's why he started writing stories instead of making things when he was young..."

My mind wasn't really on what I was telling Kate. A line from the film had just come back to me: it was what Jack had told one of his old students when he met him on a train. It was something about making sure we say the things we want to, to the people we love, before it's too late, before the moment passes and we find ourselves alone.

Suddenly I knew what I had to do. I had to see my mum and tell her how much Dad and I loved her and needed her to come back. Or else he might decide to marry Susie and it'd be too late. Then I'd be the one who'd feel all alone. I was totally sure that as soon as Dad saw Mum again, all his feelings for her would come rushing back and Susie would be history. I had to make Mum come home. Letters were no good – I couldn't even be sure she'd been getting mine.

"I'm going to London to talk to Mum," I told Kate.

"But you can't, you're too young to travel on your own!" she gasped.

"I have to, it's an emergency. You saw how Dad was with Susie today."

"Then I'm coming with you," she said firmly.

"No, you're not, *you're* far too young."

"I'm only a year younger than you. And if I don't come, I'll spend the whole time worrying about you. I'm coming and that's that."

Nothing I said could make her change her mind so we began to make plans. We worked out that the best day to go would be on Wednesday week, when Kate's school had an exceptional closure day.

"Mum works till 11 on Wednesday evenings and I have Guides, so Debbie normally comes round to make tea and put the kids to bed. She leaves after they've gone to sleep as Dad's always in the house, so she won't know I haven't come home. Dad goes to bed straight after tea so he won't notice either."

"But what about Eileen? Won't she see you're not in bed when she gets in?"

"Normally she's so shattered, she falls asleep in her chair. She probably won't find out I'm gone till the morning. But by the time she gets in, we'll be with your mum and I can phone to say we're OK."

"Won't Debbie be expecting you home for tea on Wednesday?"

"I can leave a note saying I'm having tea with you, which will be true."

I wasn't as bothered as Kate about telling a lie. I would just tell Dad I was going to a mate's house for tea and sleeping over.

Straight after school on Monday I went down to the library to check out flights on the Internet. First I went on Google to see what airlines flew from Belfast to London. When I'd got the hang of the websites, I found there were quite a few flights going to different London airports next Wednesday afternoon, but they were all quite expensive. I worked out that I had just about enough money in my savings account to pay for return flights for Kate and me. We'd need more for food and for buses or trains when we got there, but we could worry about that later. I needed to book the flights in case the price went up even more. I couldn't pay by credit card since I was too young to have one, but surely the airline must have an office somewhere, where you could take or post the money to.

I started to read through all the boring small print on the website with the cheapest flight, trying to find an address, but was stopped in my tracks by a statement saying children under fourteen must be accompanied on flights by an adult. What now? We could hardly tell any of the adults we knew what we were planning to do and ask them to come with us! After staring blankly at the screen for a few minutes, I remembered Andy, my mate Tommy's brother. He was always going to London to see his girlfriend and he owed me a favour for finding his credit card. Maybe he wouldn't mind taking a wee trip over with us next week. I logged off the computer and headed round to Tommy's house to see if Andy was there.

Tommy's mum came to the door. "Hello, Jack, we're just in the middle of our tea. Go on up to Tommy's room and he'll be with you as soon as he's finished."

I'd already worked out I'd have to tell Tommy the whole story, since he was bound to find out from Andy anyway. I thought I could trust him not to blab to anyone. He was a bit surprised when I told him it was really Andy I needed to speak to.

"Don't think he's planning to go over to Sheryl's anytime soon," he said. "She was over here a couple of weekends ago. Anyway, he says he's stony broke."

Still, he thought it was worth me asking, so he went to give Andy a shout. Andy's eyes narrowed as I gave him the low-down.

"Yeah, I'll come with you," he said when I'd finished. "But you'll have to pay for my flight as well. I'm skint."

"But I've hardly enough flippin' money for me and Kate!" I told him. "I just thought you might've been thinking of going over to London anyway and we could tag along."

"Well I wasn't, much as I would like to." Andy got up. "That's the deal. You pay for my flight; I'll be your babysitter. Take it or leave it."

"OK then, I'll pay," I said quickly, knowing we couldn't do it without him. "But you'll have to give me a few days to find some more cash."

"Tell you what, since I owe you a favour, I'll go down to the library and book the flights on my credit card tonight," Andy said. "It's cheaper to do it online. Tomorrow you can bring me the money you've already got and I'll need the rest by the day before we go. If I don't have it by then, I'll be flying out on my own. Understand?"

"I'll get the money," I told him, already trying to work out how.

"How much more do we need?" Kate asked when I came to her house after school next day to tell her the bad news.

"Only about £150!" I groaned. "Andy's flight costs over £70 and we have to make sure we've enough for bus fares and things when we get there."

"It'd be better if I wasn't coming, wouldn't it?" Kate said quietly. "Then you'd only have to pay for you and Andy."

"It's too late now, we're all booked," I said. "Anyway I'm kind of glad you're coming to keep me company. The whole thing's getting a bit scary, now it's only a week away."

"You're sure?" Kate said, brightening up. "Well, I'm going to ask Mum for money for my birthday. It won't be much but it'll help a bit."

"But you're getting a phone for your birthday!" Kate had wanted a mobile for ages and her mum had seen one on special offer.

"No, Mum hasn't bought it yet. They're holding it over till she gets paid on Thursday. I'll just tell her I've changed my mind and want the money instead. Please, Jack, I really want to help."

Well, if Kate could make a sacrifice like that, then so could I. I couldn't sell my mobile as we might need it when we got to London, but the next afternoon I took my PlayStation down to the games store in the shopping centre and traded it in for cash. I also sold my games, including the one Mum had bought me for Christmas. This hurt, but there was no point keeping it when I'd nothing to play it on and I was sure Mum would understand.

By now we'd enough money to pay for Andy's flight and a bit left over for extras. I looked up a bus route planner on the Internet to see how to get to Mum's address from the centre of London and then tried to work out how much we'd need for bus and train fares. We probably had just about enough to cover these, but it would be tight and we'd have to manage on sandwiches brought from home until we reached Mum's house. Once we'd met up with her, we'd be OK. I was sure she'd lend us the money to get back to the airport. Hopefully we'd all be travelling there together.

"Sorry I haven't bought you a present this year," I whispered to Kate when Dad and I went round for Sunday dinner to celebrate her birthday, which had been on Friday. I'd made her a card myself as I couldn't afford to waste any money at all.

"That's OK, you can buy me a really dear one next year!" she grinned back.

When we got home, Dad took some notes from his wallet.

"I didn't realise you hadn't enough money to buy Kate a present, son. Sorry your pocket money hasn't been too regular recently, but I've got back into the way of working again. I've just got paid for a big job. Take this and get something you really want."

"Thanks," I said, fingering the five £10 notes. Now we should have enough cash to cover any emergencies in London.

"Jack …" Dad began, but I cut him off.

"Gotta go, big test tomorrow. Thanks again," I said and escaped upstairs.

Dad and I hadn't talked much since that Saturday in Newcastle. I think he felt bad about asking Susie without telling me, and so he should! But there was no point trying to talk about it. If my plans for bringing Mum back from London worked as well as I hoped, Susie would soon be right out of the picture.

Though I was cross with my Dad, I couldn't help feeling sad we weren't getting on as well as we used to. For some reason I thought of CS Lewis and his dad, Albert. Jack had gone to Oxford University to study in 1917, but had only been there for a short time when he started to train as an officer to fight in the First World War. A few days before he went to France, he sent a telegram to Albert saying when he was leaving and hoping Albert would come to say goodbye. Albert didn't, because he hated leaving home, and Jack was really hurt. Albert didn't even come to see Jack when he was recovering in England after nearly being killed in battle. He was always very pleased when Jack came home to Little Lea for his holidays, but Jack never really liked spending time with his dad and got out of going when he could.

I hoped my Dad and I wouldn't end up like that, but once Mum and Dad were back together, things were bound to be better between us.

I added the notes Dad had given me to the rest of the cash at the bottom of my underwear drawer. Now we had enough money, all we had to do was wait for Wednesday and hope nothing messed up our plan!

Chapter 8

Our flight was due to leave the International Airport at 4.30 on Wednesday afternoon. The three of us had arranged to be at the bus station in the city centre by 2pm, to leave ourselves plenty of time to get there. I'd set off for school in my uniform that morning as Dad was still at home, but cycled back at 9.30am when I knew he'd have left for work. I changed out of my uniform and hid it in a bag at the bottom of my wardrobe, then checked my backpack to make sure I had all the maps and timetables I'd printed off the Internet. I'd ended up doing this in school instead of at the library, as the library only had one main printer and Mrs Armstrong or one of the others might have noticed my printouts and started asking questions.

Around one, I went down to the kitchen and forced myself to eat a couple of cheese rolls, though my stomach was churning. After tidying away my cup and plate and wiping the crumbs off the table, I quietly let myself out of the house. I passed the bus stop at the end of our street as I didn't want any neighbours wondering why I wasn't at school, and walked to one about five minutes down the road.

When I reached the bus station, Kate and Andy were already there. I'd thought it best if I travelled from our end of town separately from Kate in case we were spotted by anyone we knew. Andy had agreed to come in on the same bus as Kate to make sure she was OK, though not to sit too near her. We'd sit in different places on the airport bus too, just to be on the safe side. Once we were on the plane, it wouldn't matter so much. We'd be on our way and I couldn't see the pilot turning back just to bring us home!

But first, the three of us had to check in at the airport together. Andy had the printout with our booking number and the woman on the desk took it and checked her computer screen.

"Andrew Johnston, Jack Bryans, Katherine Bryans. How many bags are you checking in? Did you pack them yourselves?"

Our backpacks travelled along the conveyor belt and disappeared behind her.

"These are your boarding passes," the woman said, handing some cards to Andy. "All the flights into Gatwick today have been delayed because of morning fog. Yours is now due to leave at 5.45pm, but check the screens for any further changes."

I hadn't expected this. If the flight was nearly two hours late leaving, we wouldn't get into Gatwick until around seven o'clock. We would then have to get a coach into the centre of London and another bus out to the east of the city, where Mum lived. At this rate we wouldn't be with Mum until late in the evening. As soon as we'd passed through Security, I sat down in the departure lounge and got out my bus timetables to try to replan our journey.

In the end, we weren't called to board the plane until just before seven. By this time I was getting really worried. I wouldn't have brought Kate if I'd thought the two of us would be getting into London so late. I just hoped the streets in Mum's area were safe.

Kate was just excited at being on a plane for the first time. She grabbed my arm tightly as we came to the end of the runway and started to climb into the air, but once the plane had levelled itself, she began to relax and point out the window at the lights on the ground far below.

We reached Gatwick around 8.15pm, but it took another half hour or so to get into the airport building and pick up our luggage.

"There's Sheryl," Andy said, hoisting his bag onto his shoulder and waving back at a girl with a black ponytail. "She said she'd try to borrow her brother's car to come and meet me."

"Any chance of a lift?" I asked hopefully.

"Sorry, mate. I don't really want two kids tagging along when I meet up with my girlfriend. See you back here on Friday night."

Andy hadn't been much help, but when he'd gone, it suddenly hit me that we didn't have an adult to turn to any more. Kate and I were two kids in London on our own. I tried to pull myself together. I couldn't show Kate how scared I was. We needed to find a coach going to the centre of London. There was one due to leave at five past nine. I grabbed Kate's hand and pulled her towards the exit.

The coach was faster than my timetable had said and we reached the station in the city centre by 10.20pm. I knew the number of the bus we needed to catch to get to a stop in the East End, a few streets away from where Mum lived, so I rushed over to a ticket kiosk and asked where to wait for it. The bus was already there, and after about half an hour we got off at the 16th stop on the route. I opened the street map I'd brought with me.

"This way," I told Kate confidently.

As we walked towards the address Mum had sent me so many weeks ago, we passed a lot of older teenagers, hanging around in groups on street corners. I tried to look relaxed, as if I was as used to the area as they were. I didn't want Kate to know how I really felt. By now she was looking tired out.

"Mum will be home from work by now," she said, looking at her watch. "I just hope she hasn't noticed I'm not in bed."

"Well we can give her a ring as soon as we get to my mum's house and let her know we're both OK," I said cheerfully. "Look, here we are – Somerville Road. Number 7 must be just up there."

I held my breath as we stood on the doorstep and rang the bell. No one appeared, though there were lights on upstairs. Mum might already have gone to bed. I just hoped she hadn't gone out for the evening. I pressed the doorbell again. This time, after a few minutes, the hall suddenly lit up and we could see a shadowy figure behind the frosted glass. The door opened a chink and a woman's face appeared. It wasn't Mum's.

"What do you kids want at this time of night?" the woman demanded. "You should both be in your beds long ago!"

"We… we were looking for my mum, Caroline Bryans," I said. "We thought she lived here."

"Oh, Caroline!" the woman said, closing over the door. I thought she was shutting it in our faces, but it turned out she was just taking off a chain. When she opened the door properly, we could see she was quite old and wearing a dressing gown. We must have got her out of bed.

"Caroline did have a room here for a few months," she told us, "but she left a week ago for a new job in Oxford. She gave me the address so I could send on her post. I'll get it for you."

She disappeared into one of the rooms inside. I looked at Kate. She was making a big effort not to burst into tears. I knew I had to do the same.

"Don't worry," I told her. "Oxford's not too far from London. Remember in *Shadowlands* when Joy and Douglas went by train from London to visit Jack and Warnie?" Who'd have thought my CS Lewis project would come in so useful?

"I'm OK," Kate said. "At least your mum left her address. We'll find her, Jack, I know we will. We've two whole days, remember?"

"Do you have somewhere to stay tonight?" asked the woman, coming back with a piece of paper. She didn't seem too keen to ask us in.

"N...," Kate began.

"Yes, we do," I cut in. "We're going there now. Thanks very much for this. Bye."

"Why did you tell her that?" Kate asked, as we walked back down the street.

"Well, we couldn't let her know we've nowhere to stay or she'd phone the police."

We went into a chip shop and asked the man behind the counter the best way to get to Oxford. He gave us a hard stare, but there was a queue of proper customers forming behind us.

"You need to get to Paddington Station," he said quickly. "It'll take you an hour or so. First you'll have to catch a bus from the stop across the road, and when you reach Whitechapel, you'll need to go on the Underground."

This was all turning into a bit of a nightmare, but we couldn't give up now. I was very glad we had the money Dad had given me for all these extra fares. We waited quite a while for the bus, but the driver was very helpful and when he heard we'd never used the Underground before, he told us exactly where to go and what to do.

"Hope your mum's there when you get to Paddington!" he called after us. I tried not to look at Kate. I'd sort of hinted to the driver we were meeting Mum there, but what else could I do? He was concerned about us travelling alone so late at night and if he'd thought no one was meeting us, he'd probably have called the police.

When we got off the Underground at Paddington and asked about trains for Oxford, we were told the last one had just left. Flippin' typical. The next one was at 5.20 in the morning.

"Well, we need to have a rest and we don't really want to be looking around Oxford for Mum in the middle of the night," I said, trying to cheer us both up. We walked around a bit, trying to find a bench that was out of sight of any of the people who worked at the station. Eventually we found one and plonked ourselves down on it.

"You get some sleep. I'm not all that tired so I'll stay awake and watch our stuff."

"No, we'll take turns," she insisted. "Promise you'll wake me in a couple of hours."

"OK," I said, knowing I wouldn't.

We ate the rest of the sandwiches we'd brought and drank some hot chocolate from a drinks machine, then Kate leaned against my shoulder and fell asleep straight away.

This was the first chance I'd had to think through what had happened and try to plan what we would do once we got to Oxford. I couldn't believe Mum had moved house without letting me know. Maybe she just wanted to disappear out of our lives altogether! Well I wasn't going to let that happen. If we got the early train to Oxford, we'd hopefully be with her before she left for work in the morning.

At first it wasn't hard to stay awake, I felt so hacked off about everything. I didn't know who I was angriest with – Mum for going off again without telling me, Dad for trying to replace Mum, or God for letting all this happen. But after a while I felt myself drifting off. Next thing I knew, Kate was shaking me hard.

"Jack, wake up! It's after nine o'clock!"

How could I have let myself fall asleep when we needed to get to Oxford as early as possible? I rubbed my eyes and grabbed the railway timetable.

"There's a train in five minutes. Get your bag and run!"

A short time later we were facing each other in a railway carriage, hurtling through the English countryside. It was funny to think of CS Lewis passing the same trees and fields all those years ago when he travelled between London and Oxford by steam train. When Kate and I were watching *Shadowlands* the other Saturday, we'd certainly never thought we'd be visiting Oxford ourselves so soon.

Halfway through the journey, a text came through on my mobile.

"From Susie," I said. The message read, "Jack where r u. Ur dads going crazy, Kate's mum and dad 2. Pls ring. S."

"Please can we phone and let them know we're safe?" Kate begged.

"Not yet." I didn't want anyone at home butting in before we'd reached Mum. "We need to find Mum first and then we'll ring." I turned off the phone and put it back in my pocket.

The train pulled into Oxford Station at 10.30am and we walked out onto a crowded street. As we stood wondering

what to do next, a whoosh of cyclists passed us, with
striped scarves waving out behind them in the breeze.
Students on their way to college, probably. Everyone but
us seemed to know where they were going.

"Right, we need to get a map." I said.

"There's a signpost for Tourist Information," Kate
pointed.

But the maps in the Information Office were only of the
centre of Oxford.

"Do you know where this street is?" I asked the girl
behind the desk, showing her the piece of paper we'd
been given last night.

"Let's see, hmm, I think that's in Wolvercote," the girl
said. "My aunt lives there. You'll need to get a bus from
the station, right beside the train station."

"Let's go straight there." I said to Kate, as we left.
"Even if Mum's gone to work when we find the house, at
least we'll know we're at the right place."

"No, first we need to get some breakfast," Kate replied
firmly. "We haven't had a proper meal since we left
home."

She was right. We didn't know how long it would take
to find Mum's house and I was starting to feel a bit dizzy.
A familiar, very modern smell was wafting down the
street, in contrast to the old buildings all around.

"Over there, a KFC!" I grinned. "That shouldn't cost
too much."

It seemed a bit strange to be scoffing fried chicken and
chips at 11 o'clock in the morning, but we both felt a lot
better when we came back outside. We'd decided to get
the bus out to Wolvercote and ask the driver to let us out
at the right stop.

"Kingfisher Walk?" he said, frowning at the address. "I think that might be near St Peter's Road, but I can't be sure."

"That's all right, let us out as close as you can to St Peter's Road, and we'll ask someone," I said, moving on up the bus.

No one we asked seemed to have heard of Kingfisher Walk, though they gave us plenty of suggestions. We spent over an hour wandering around before stopping for a drink in a cafe.

"You're in the wrong part of Oxford altogether," the waitress there finally told us. "Kingfisher Walk isn't far from where I used to live, in Blackbird Leys."

On the other side of the paper with Mum's address on it she wrote down the number of the right bus and sketched a map of the streets around the bus stop, marking Kingfisher Walk quite clearly.

"Thanks so much," I said, leaping up from the table and handing her a couple of pounds. "Keep the change."

At last we were on the right track. Around two-thirty we got off *another* bus and looked at the map the waitress had drawn. We needed to head up the next street on the right and turn left at the Chinese takeaway on the corner.

"We should be there in a couple of minutes," I smiled at Kate. "As soon as we get there, we'll phone home and let everyone know we're OK."

"Jack," Kate said in a strange voice, "I think that car's following us."

As I turned round to look, the car pulled up at the kerb and a big policeman jumped out from the front passenger seat.

"I don't think you kids should go wandering off again," he said sternly. "There's someone here who needs to talk to you."

Surely we couldn't be arrested just for running away.
But the policeman did look very serious. The back door of
the car swung open and someone got out.

"Mum!" I gasped against the rough wool of her coat, as
she folded me in her arms.

Chapter 9

After the police had dropped us off at Mum's flat, which was only about a minute's drive from where they'd picked us up, the first thing Mum made us do was phone home to say we were safe. I thought it was better if Kate called Eileen and got her to tell Dad, as I didn't really want to talk to him until I found out how likely it was that Mum would be coming home.

Kate came out of Mum's bedroom, where the phone was, in tears. "We should have rung them this morning when we were on our way to Oxford. They've all been going up the walls. Mum could hardly speak to me."

She sipped at a glass of milk my mum had set in front of her, along with a plate of sandwiches, and for a few moments none of us knew what to say. I was thinking to myself that if we'd met up with Mum last night as I'd planned, no one at home would have been nearly as worried. At last I couldn't keep this in any longer.

"Why didn't you let us know you'd moved?" I demanded.

"But I did," Mum said, surprised. "I sent you an email the day after I arrived here."

I'd been so busy planning our trip to London that I hadn't remembered to check my emails recently. Anyway, I'd given up hope of getting any from Mum.

"But you never emailed me before, even though I kept asking you to!" I said. "I know you couldn't write to me in case Dad found out, but I told you he wouldn't know if you emailed me."

Mum sighed. "Oh Jack. You were bombarding me with so many letters, asking me to come back, that I couldn't think straight. I still needed space to work out what was best for our family. I know now I should have contacted you more often, but I found it hard to know the answers to the questions you were asking me."

I didn't know what to say to that. I'd thought it was important to be honest with her.

"How did the police find out where we were?" Kate asked, a bit less tearfully.

"When your mum called you for school this morning and discovered you weren't in your room, she phoned Mike, who called Rick's house to speak to Jack because he thought he'd been spending the night there. Rick knew nothing about this so Mike got in touch with some of Jack's other friends. He eventually found out from Tommy that you'd both gone to London with his brother. Mike realised you must have gone looking for me and called the police. They must have got my address in London from Mrs King. She was the only person back home, apart from you, Jack, who knew what it was."

"So did the police in London look for us there?" I asked.

"Yes, and Miss Trimble, the landlady, told them you'd been there late yesterday evening and that she'd given you my new address in Oxford. Apparently they gave her a lecture about not keeping you there and phoning for them to come straight away."

"I think she just wanted to get back to bed," I said. "And I did tell her we had somewhere to stay last night."

"By the time the police in Oxford were contacted, it was lunchtime. They came here and the woman in the flat upstairs, who I've got to know a bit, was able to tell them where I worked. They picked me up from the office and we drove around for quite a while until we found you."

"Why did you move to Oxford anyway?" I asked. "I'd have thought living in London would be much more exciting."

"When I was young, I'd always dreamed of going to university here," she explained. "My d... someone I knew had told me a lot about it and it seemed like a fairytale place to me. Of course, I ended up leaving school without even taking A levels and for a long time I forgot about my dream. After I'd been working in London for a few months, I saw an advert for a job here in Oxford and I thought it would be a chance to live here for a while and maybe do some exams. I've signed up for a couple of courses at the local Further Education College, and who knows? I might end up going to university some day. Probably not here in Oxford, but I suppose you never know."

It didn't sound as if she was thinking of coming home anytime soon.

"Queen's in Belfast is meant to be a good university," I said, remembering what I'd heard one of my teachers at school say. But before Mum could reply, the doorbell rang.

"I'll get it," I said, glad to get out of the room for a minute.

I went into the tiny hallway and turned the handle. A stout old man was standing outside, dressed in a tweed suit and hat. I took a step back in amazement. It was CS Lewis!

Mum had followed me out of the living room and saw the figure on the doorstep just a second after I did.

"Dad?" she said, looking as if she was about to faint.

"Hello, Caroline," the old man smiled, though I could see there were tears in his eyes. "We came over as soon as we heard the children were here. Would it be all right if we came in?"

"I suppose so," Mum said, not sounding very sure. We both stood back to let the door open fully and it was only then I realised someone else had been standing behind the first man, on the step below. I darted back into the living room.

"You'll never believe this, Kate," I whispered. "Your dad's here!"

Mum mumbled something about making a pot of tea and disappeared into the kitchen. Kate and Billy sat on the sofa, crying and hugging. Mum's dad (*my other grandfather*, I suddenly realised) and I perched on the edges of the other two chairs, looking shyly at one another.

At last the old man said, "I'm sorry for surprising you like that, Jack. It must be very strange to come face to face with a grandfather you've never met before."

I explained it wasn't that which had shocked me so much; it was because he'd reminded me of the pictures I'd seen of CS Lewis.

He gave a deep chuckle. "I suppose I *am* dressed in the sort of clothes he used to wear. I knew him, you know. He was my tutor when I was studying English Literature here in Oxford in the early 1950s, before he went to be a Professor at Cambridge University. But I'm not really much like him, apart from being on the plump side. He was quite a bit taller than me, with a red face, and black hair – what was left of it. Of course, I'm a good bit older than he was when he died, just before he was 65. People used to think he looked more like a big burly farmer than a lecturer or a writer."

Now he'd taken off his hat to reveal a head of thick white hair, I could see he was right. He didn't look much like CS Lewis at all, apart from the clothes.

"Did you get to know him well?" I asked, glad we'd found something to talk about.

"I used to stay behind for a chat after tutorials from time to time. My parents sent me a newspaper from home once a month and he was always keen to see it. He never lost interest in what was happening in Belfast and always referred to Northern Ireland as 'home'. He also encouraged me when I told him I was thinking of studying to become a minister."

"I'm doing a project about him for school," I said. "Maybe I could interview you." It would be cool to do a piece on someone who'd actually known CS Lewis, especially someone related to me!

"I'd be delighted," he smiled. "As long as it's OK with Caroline."

Mum pushed through the kitchen door with a tray of mugs and some biscuits. When the grown-ups were sitting back with their tea and Kate and I were munching custard creams, Billy began to explain how they both came to be there.

"Eileen called Kate at 7.30 this morning and discovered she hadn't slept in her bed, so she shook me awake. It took me a while to come to – I'm always worse in the mornings. By the time I did, Eileen had phoned Mike and they'd realised Jack wasn't at his friend's house like he'd said. I got dressed and we went straight up to Mike's. Mike was ringing round all your friends, Jack, and at last found out from Tommy that you'd gone to London with his brother. We knew you'd probably gone to find Caroline, but nobody knew where she lived. While the police were on their way, Mike thought it might be worth phoning your parents, Caroline, just in case you'd been in touch with them at any stage since you'd left."

Mum raised her eyebrows at this and her dad said quietly, "Of course, you hadn't been. We hadn't heard from you in over 13 years, but Mike didn't know what else to do. Eileen thought they still had your phone number in their book, so Billy went back down to their house to phone us. Helen and I were extremely concerned that Jack and Kate were missing, so we got in the car and came straight over to Mike's to see if we could do anything to help."

Billy took up the story again. "By the time Adrian and Helen arrived, two policemen were there. They'd got in touch with the London police, who were trying to find out if anyone had any idea where you'd gone after leaving the airport. Then Mrs King from next door came in. She'd seen the police car outside and wondered what was wrong. She was able to give the police Caroline's address in London and they passed it on to the policemen who were looking for you there. We knew that when you were found, someone would have to go over and bring you home. Mike wanted to go, of course, but didn't know how Caroline would react to seeing him, so Adrian volunteered to go instead, and I said I would go with him because of Kate. We managed to get seats on the next flight out and as soon as we landed, we phoned home to find out if there'd been any news. Eileen said the police had let her know you were safe and sound in Oxford, and had given her Caroline's address. She also said Kate had been on the phone but she'd been so overcome to hear from her that she'd forgotten to tell her I was over here!

Adrian hired a car at the airport and we got here as soon as we could."

"I need time to talk to Jack," Mum said. "You're not planning to take them back straight away?"

"No, of course not," her dad said. "Did you book a return flight, Jack and Kate?"

"Yes, tomorrow evening," I told him.

"Well then, if you give me the details, we'll see if we can get booked on the same flight. In the meantime, I know of a very good little guest house a few miles from here, where Billy and I can stay with Kate. That'll give you and your mum time on your own to catch up."

"Thanks," my mum said, smiling weakly at her dad for the first time.

"If we can just have your number, we'll give you a ring tomorrow morning to let you know what's happening with the flights," her dad said, standing up along with Billy and Kate and moving towards the door.

"Bye, Jack," Kate said. She was holding her dad's hand and looking very happy.

"See you, Kate," I replied, suddenly nervous about being on my own with Mum. I'd been hoping to persuade her to come back with us tomorrow evening but now the time had come, I hardly knew what to say.

"Well, I've made a right mess of things, haven't I?" Mum said, slumping on the sofa once she'd closed the door on the others.

"What do you mean?" My anger with Mum had died down after what she'd said about my letters getting her all mixed up. "It was us who caused all the fuss and made everyone so worried, well me. Kate only went along with it to keep me company."

"No, it wasn't your fault, Jack," Mum said. "It was me who made the big mistake all those years ago, getting together with your dad just to make my parents pay more attention to me. Things were fine when I was younger. I loved my mum and absolutely hero-worshipped my dad because of all the things he did to help other people. I heard you talking to him about CS Lewis, so you've probably worked out by now it was because Dad went to Oxford University that I started to dream of going there one day too.

"Then, when I became a teenager, all of a sudden my parents didn't seem to know how to handle me. I know all parents and teenagers feel at times they don't understand each other, but mine found it much more difficult because they were a lot older than my friends' parents. They used to send me on holiday with my friends' families while they would go off somewhere by themselves, just the two of them. I see now it was because they thought I would have more fun with younger people, but at the time I thought they just wanted to get rid of me. So as I got older, I tried to shock them into noticing me. I began to resent all the time they gave to other people in their work at the church. When I started going out with your dad and shortly afterwards announced we were going to get engaged, I thought at last, they'd put their foot down. But they just accepted it, even though I knew they wanted other things for me. So, to get back at them, I ended up going through with it. I hadn't seen my dad since the day before we ran away to get married, until today. It was quite a shock, I can tell you."

So Dad had been right. The main reason Mum had married him was to get back at her parents.

"So didn't you love Dad at all?" Thinking of Dad's love not being returned, made *me* hurt inside.

"Come over here beside me, Jack."

I joined Mum on the sofa and she put an arm around me. "I know this is hard for you to hear, but you're growing up and I want you to understand why I felt in the end I had to leave you. At first I thought I did love your dad. He was so good-looking and all the girls were crazy about him. I was really flattered when he picked me out of all the others he could have had. But shortly after we got married, I realised I'd made the biggest mistake of my life and was never going to achieve all the ambitions I'd once had of going to Oxford and having a career. I thought if I had a baby, things would improve – at least I would have someone I could really love."

"Was I part of the mistake then?" I asked. I could tell I was about to cry.

Mum gave me a big hug. "Oh no, love, you were no mistake. Like I said in the note I left, you were the best thing that ever happened to me. I didn't know the meaning of love until you were born. And for a while things were better between your dad and me, because we both doted on you. Then, after a couple of years, I began to see that apart from you, we didn't have much in common. If it hadn't been for you, I would never have stayed with him as long as I did, but I didn't want you to grow up in a home without both parents. There were times I felt so trapped I thought of taking you and moving out, but I knew that would have ripped out your dad's heart; he was so crazy about you. That's why I was such a hopeless mother. I knew I needed to leave for my own sake. But for your sake, and your dad's, I just couldn't do it, so I ended up being depressed a lot of the time. Then, last summer, after I'd got that job and wasn't moping around the house so much, I began to realise we couldn't go on as we were.

"I knew that over the years your dad had been a far better parent to you than I had, so I thought it best to leave you with him while I went away to think everything through. I'm sorry I left without telling you, but I knew if I tried to explain things to your dad, he would try to stop me going and I probably wouldn't have had the strength to carry through my plan. That's why I just left you both notes. When I got to London, I found it hard to settle, even though I eventually made a few friends through work. It's only in the short time since I've been in Oxford that my mind's really started to clear and I've realised that I might be happy living here. I was planning to ring your dad next week and ask if he would let you come over for part of the Easter holidays."

So even if Mum didn't come home with us, I would see her again soon. Easter was less than three weeks away.

"There's something you'd better know before you talk to Dad." I took a deep breath and told Mum about Susie.

She seemed a bit shocked, but said she was glad Dad had found someone who made him happy. After that we ordered pizza. Then Mum made up a bed for me on the sofa and kissed me goodnight.

My head was full of so much stuff I didn't think I'd sleep, but as I lay in the dark, listening to Mum moving about in the kitchen, I realised I felt more peaceful than I had in months, even though it didn't look as if Mum and Dad would be getting back together. Was it because I was starting to understand why they'd acted like they had and I didn't feel mad at them any more?

But before my mind could answer that question, I fell asleep.

Chapter 10

Just after eight the next morning, Mum woke me.

"Your grandpa's on the phone – Billy, I mean," she said.

I went into Mum's room and lifted the phone from where she'd left it, face up on the bed.

"Morning, Jack. Hope you slept well. Just to let you know we've been able to get seats on the same flight as you this evening. Oh, and Adrian wants to know if you and Caroline would like to come on a tour of Oxford. He thinks it might be helpful for your project if you saw some of the places to do with CS Lewis."

"Hang on a minute," I said, laying down the phone again. Mum was in the kitchen buttering toast and I told her what Billy had said.

"I'm really sorry Jack, but I have to go to work this morning. I've only just started this job and I had to leave at lunchtime yesterday when the police came. You go with the others and I'll see if I can get away a bit earlier than usual. Ask Billy if he and Kate and… my dad would like to come here for an early dinner, say about five. Your flight's not until nearly ten o' clock, so that'll leave you plenty of time to get to the airport."

I was disappointed not to be spending the whole day with Mum but reminded myself that we'd have lots of time together over Easter. And it *would* be a good chance to find out more about CS Lewis' life in Oxford, as well as getting to know my new grandfather. I repeated mum's words to Billy and he said they'd pick me up in an hour.

"I can't believe the change in your dad," I whispered to Kate. We were sitting together in the back of the car, slowly approaching the centre of Oxford.

"Isn't it fantastic?" Kate beamed back. "He said the shock of us disappearing made him wise up and see what was really important."

We managed to find a space in a car park close to the train station.

"I don't know what to call you," I told my mum's dad as I walked beside him towards the colleges. Kate was behind us, holding her dad's hand tightly.

"Well, let's see." He thought for a moment. "You don't call Billy Grandad or Grandpa or anything like that, and you've known him a lot longer than you've known me, so I think it will have to be Adrian – for the time being at least."

First of all, Adrian took us past the shopping streets where Kate and I had been yesterday, and pointed to a house on the corner of Mansfield Road.

"That was the first place CS Lewis stayed in Oxford while he was doing his entrance exams in 1916," he said. "He'd come up from Surrey where he was being tutored by a man called Kirkpatrick whom CSL called..."

"The Great Knock!" I finished. I remembered reading this somewhere.

"That's right. Did you know that the character of Professor Kirke in *The Lion, the Witch and the Wardrobe* was based on him? CSL learned more in the two and a half years he lived with Kirkpatrick than in all his time at school. One of the most important things Kirkpatrick taught him was how to argue a point logically. This proved to be very useful later, in his teaching and writings."

The next building Adrian pointed out was University College where CS Lewis came as a student in 1917. Soon after starting, he had volunteered for active duty in the First World War but returned in 1919 to continue his studies. He turned out to be one of the cleverest people in his year, gaining top degrees in both Classics and English Literature.

"I've never seen buildings that colour before," Kate remarked.

I could see what she meant. The stone most of the colleges seemed to be made of was sort of honey-coloured.

We carried on walking for quite a while until we saw a tower rising in front of us. "This is the famous tower of Magdalen College," Adrian told us, "where CS Lewis taught for nearly thirty years and where, much less importantly, I was a student for four years."

Adrian took us past the tower and up onto Magdalen Bridge, from where we could look down on the wee boats bobbing about on the Cherwell River.

"Not many punts on the river today," Adrian said, "but in another couple of months, there'll be a queue of people waiting to hire them. CSL enjoyed boating on the river in the summer, and swimming in it as well. Now let's go into the College itself."

Inside the grounds of Magdalen (which for some reason was pronounced "Maud–lin"), Adrian showed us the staircase up to the room he'd stayed in as a student and the windows of the rooms Jack had lived and taught in during his time there.

"He only lived there during the week in term time," Adrian said. "At weekends and in the holidays he had a house of his own about three miles away. I've made an appointment for us to see round it this afternoon."

At the back of the building where CS Lewis had his rooms there was a huge green area.

"Look, what's that over there?" exclaimed Kate, spotting something moving behind a fence.

"It's a deer," Adrian said. "CSL had a view of this park from his room – imagine looking out on this every morning!"

As we moved closer to the fence, we could see there were lots of deer, including a couple of wobbly-legged fawns. We stayed for a while, watching them nibble the grass, before heading down to a path that ran along the river.

"This is known as Addison's Walk," said Adrian. "Strolling along here one night, CS Lewis had one of the most important conversations of his life, with two of his closest friends, Hugo Dyson and JRR Tolkien."

"The author of *The Lord of the Rings*?" I asked.

"The very same!" Adrian smiled. "Later on, he and CSL encouraged each other to write the sort of books they both liked reading. *The Lord of the Rings* would probably never have been published if CSL hadn't nagged Tolkien into finishing it, because he thought it was so good. Sadly, Tolkien was less enthusiastic about *The Lion, the Witch and the Wardrobe*. But that was a few years later. On the night they walked here in 1931, Tolkien and Dyson, who were both Christians, were challenging CSL on why he found it so hard to accept that Jesus was the Son of God and this got him thinking. A week or so after this conversation he travelled to Whipsnade Zoo in the sidecar of his brother's motorbike. By the time they got there CSL had come to believe that Jesus really was God's Son, sent to earth by God to take the punishment human beings deserved for all their wrong thoughts and actions. It was the major turning point in his life and in his writing... Now, if anyone's feeling hungry, I've thought of somewhere rather special where we can have lunch."

We were all hungry after so much walking, and even hungrier by the time we reached the pub where Adrian had decided we would eat.

On the sign outside, there was a painting of a small child in the claws of a big bird. ("Scar–y," murmured Kate.)

"Welcome to The Eagle and Child," Adrian said, holding open the door as the rest of us passed through, "known to locals as 'The Bird and Baby'. It was here CSL used to meet up with Tolkien and some other friends who were interested in writing, to read out extracts from the books they were working on."

It was still quite early for lunch and we'd no trouble getting a table in the part of the pub where "The Inklings", as Jack's group of friends called themselves, used to meet. On the wood-panelled walls there were photos of some of them and a framed list of their signatures. I could see Jack's and Tolkien's among them. It felt quite spooky to be having lunch in the very place where bits from *The Lord of the Rings* and the *Narnia* stories had first been read out.

Billy didn't seem at all spooked.

"Now this is more my sort of place," he sighed happily, sinking into a padded chair. "All that learning and culture back there was a bit over my head. I was only fifteen when I left school and went to work in the shipyard, remember! You wouldn't be offended, Adrian, if I ordered a pint?"

"Go ahead," Adrian said, as a waitress approached our table. "Would you children like Coke with your lunch?"

After filling up on toasted sandwiches and chocolate cake, we were ready to walk back to the car. Our appointment at The Kilns, the house where CS Lewis had lived for most of his time in Oxford, wasn't until 2.30pm. This gave us time to explore the woods behind the house, which were now open to the public.

"The woods are all that's left of the grounds which once belonged to the house," Adrian explained. "The rest was sold off for housing development after Warnie Lewis died in the early 1970s."

Near the entrance to the woods was a big pond, which Jack used to punt and swim in. There were other smaller ponds further up the hill, between the trees. They reminded me of the pools in "the Wood between the Worlds" in *The Magicians' Nephew*, which Polly and Digory jump into to get from one world to another, with the help of the magic rings.

"We'd better get going!" Adrian called from the seat beside the main pond where he and Billy had been resting. Kate and I scrambled back down the hill to join them.

As we got closer to The Kilns, I noticed it looked quite like Little Lea, though not nearly as big. Both houses were built of red brick and had red-tiled pointed roofs, tall chimneys and windows with lots of small square panes. I wondered if this was why Jack had decided to buy The Kilns. We were met at the front door by an American lady called Louise, who explained that the house wasn't kept like a museum but was a home to people with an interest in CS Lewis, who'd come to study in Oxford for a short time. None of the furniture there now had belonged to the Lewis family, as most of their things had been sold or gone to a museum in the United States.

We did see some of Jack's pipes on the desk in the window of the living room, where he would have done some of his writing. I'd been taking lots of photos for my project with the camera on my mobile; I got a good one of

Billy sitting at the desk, pretending to smoke one of the pipes. In the dining room, Louise showed us the typewriter Warnie had used to type out the family history and to answer the letters his brother was sent from all over the world after he became famous for his books and radio broadcasts.

Louise told us that Jack and Warnie Lewis had bought the house in 1930 after their father had died and Little Lea had been sold. Mrs Moore, the mother of Jack's friend, Paddy, who'd been killed in the war, also helped to buy it.

"Before Jack and Paddy went off to fight in France, they made a pact," Louise said. "If Jack died and Paddy didn't, Paddy would look after Jack's father. If Paddy died and Jack survived, Jack would look after Paddy's mother. Jack didn't find it hard to keep his promise as he thought Minto, as he called Mrs Moore, was wonderful. She'd looked after him when he was wounded and his own father hadn't come to visit him. At first life was tough, with Jack, Mrs Moore and her daughter, Maureen, all trying to live on the student allowance Jack was given by his father, Albert."

"Didn't Albert mind?" I interrupted. I remembered reading that Albert hadn't been too happy about Jack being friendly with Mrs Moore.

"Oh, Jack made sure he never found out!" Louise laughed. "When Jack got the job at Oxford, things became easier for him and the Moores. He also started to get on better with his father, because he no longer had to depend on him for money. Mrs Moore lived at The Kilns with Jack and Warnie until she became old and sick and had to go into a nursing home. Even then, Jack visited her every day until she died, keeping the promise he'd made to Paddy all those years before."

We saw the room where Joy had slept after she'd married Jack and was well enough to come home from hospital. It wasn't upstairs like in the *Shadowlands* film because she wasn't able to cope with the stairs. After Joy died and Jack himself became ill, he also had to move to a downstairs room and that was where he died in 1963.

As we all stood in that room, Adrian told us of how sad he'd been when a friend, who still lived in Oxford, phoned him with the news of their old tutor's death.

"Most of the world didn't pay much attention because it happened on the very same day John F Kennedy, the President of the United States, was assassinated. But those of us who'd known CSL or been helped by his writings felt a real sense of loss, as well as being glad that his sufferings were over and he was now in heaven."

The last thing Louise showed us was a wardrobe, which stood in the hall near the foot of the stairs. "Of course, this isn't the wardrobe that stood here in Jack's time – the one carved by his grandfather – which had come from Little Lea. That's now on display in Wheaton College in the US. The story goes that one of the convent girls who were evacuated here during the Second World War, asked Jack one day if there was anything behind the wardrobe, and that gave him the idea for the *Narnia* books."

As the children in *The Lion, the Witch and the Wardrobe* are evacuees living in Professor Kirke's house, I didn't find this too hard to believe.

"The last place we're going to visit is very close by," Adrian said, after we'd thanked Louise and got back into the car.

In a few minutes we were standing at the gates of Holy Trinity Church, where Jack and Warnie used to go on Sundays. The Lewis brothers and Mrs Moore were all buried in the churchyard. We couldn't find Mrs Moore's grave but Adrian was able to take us straight to Jack and Warnie's, which was under a tall pine tree covered in ivy. Kate and I brushed off some dead leaves from the surface of the headstone and we all stood quietly for a few moments, reading the inscriptions.

Kate pointed to the words sandwiched between the two names. "Men must endure their going hence," she read out. "What does that mean?"

"It's a quotation from Shakespeare," said Adrian. "From what I remember, it was on a calendar in Flora Lewis's room on the day she died. I don't think the brothers ever really got over their mother's death."

It was time to head back for dinner. This time I sat in the front of the car, chatting to Adrian. As we got nearer Mum's flat, he became very quiet.

"I don't want your mum thinking the real reason I came over to bring you home was to try to patch up the quarrel between us," he said as we turned into Kingfisher Walk. "That's why I didn't hang around long yesterday. Caroline always questioned our motives, no matter what her mother and I did."

"I think you need to talk," I said, knowing how much better my chat with Mum had made me feel.

"I'll suggest it," Adrian said doubtfully, "but I'm not sure she'll agree."

But in the end it was Mum who asked her dad to come into the kitchen and help her dry the dishes. We'd just finished a meal of creamy chicken and rice, which we had to eat on our knees as there was no space for a table in the room. Mum's cooking had definitely improved since she'd left home!

"Do you think they've nearly finished in there?" Billy wondered, looking at his watch. "It's time we made tracks for the airport. You never know what the traffic's going to be like."

The kitchen door opened at last and we all got our coats on, ready to say goodbye to Mum.

"We'll wait in the car, Jack, and give you a few minutes by yourselves," Adrian said, steering the others towards the door.

Mum hugged me so tight I could hardly breathe.

"I took the plunge and phoned your dad earlier, just before you got back," she said, letting me go at last. "We've arranged for you to come over here for a week, the day after you finish school. The office is closed for two days at Easter and I should be able to take a few more days off by then."

Knowing I would be seeing her again so soon made it much easier for me to leave. She came out with me to the car and waved us off.

Billy was right about the traffic. We got caught up in major road works and reached the airport about ten minutes before check-in was due to close.

After we'd handed over our luggage, we turned towards the departure lounge.

"Look over there!" I nudged Kate.

Andy and Sheryl were standing superglued together about ten metres away from the check-in desk.

"I'd forgotten all about him!" Kate laughed.

I shouted over to Andy that he was going to miss the flight and he tore himself away from Sheryl, checked in his bag just in the nick of time and sprinted after us towards Departures. He looked a bit puzzled that Kate and I seemed to have hooked up with two old men, but we didn't feel like explaining. Not yet anyway.

Our flight hadn't been called yet, so Billy took Kate into the newsagents to buy her a magazine for the plane. I followed Adrian to a row of seats nearby.

"So how did your talk with Mum go?" Their faces, when they'd come out of the kitchen, hadn't given much away.

"All right, I think," Adrian replied slowly. "We were able to clear up a few misunderstandings. She said she'd think about coming to stay with us when she flies over to visit you in the summer. If she does, maybe you could come for a few days as well."

"That'd be great." I wondered if Helen was the kind of granny who made homemade lemonade. From what Mum and Adrian had said about her, I suspected she might be.

"Do you mind if I ask you something?" I said suddenly, keeping an eye on the newsagents, where Kate was still making up her mind.

"Fire away."

"Well, you were a minister, so maybe you can tell me why, when I prayed, God didn't answer. At first it did seem as if the prayers were being answered, but the main aim of all my praying was that Mum would come home for good and no matter what way I said the words or how often I prayed it didn't work. Now it doesn't look as if she'll ever come back."

Adrian's bushy white eyebrows knit together as he thought about this. At last he said, "I think, Jack, you've discovered what CS Lewis found out many years before you. When he was a child and his mother was ill, he prayed hard that she would get better, but, as we know, she died. Later, he realised that God isn't a magician, simply there to answer our prayers in the way we demand and then disappear as soon as we get what we want."

This was exactly what I'd hoped God would do.

"So there's more to praying than that verse Kate told me, about asking and receiving?" I asked.

"Well," Adrian said, "Prayer isn't just about asking for the things we want or think we need. First, we need to put our trust in Jesus – that gives us a direct line to God. Then we need to spend time talking to God and listening to him – just getting to know him really. When we do that, we gradually learn to trust him to answer our prayers in the way that's best for us and for everyone else we're praying for. The answer we receive might be an instant 'yes', which is wonderful, it might be a definite 'no' and we may never know the reason why, or it might be 'wait'."

I made a face at this and Adrian laughed.

"Yes, that can be the hardest answer of all, as your grandmother and I know only too well from all our years of praying that we might be reconciled with your mum. Now, at long last, it looks as if we're moving in the right direction, but I've a feeling we might have to wait a bit longer before our prayers are finally answered."

I thought about this while Adrian went to buy a paper. What he'd said was maybe like the thing in the *Narnia* books that had been bugging me – the idea that though Aslan isn't *safe*, he is *good*. For the first time I thought I understood a bit about what CS Lewis might have meant by this. We want to keep the people we love close to us so we know we're safe, but sometimes things don't work out that way and that's when we need to remember Aslan is good. What was I saying? Aslan was just a talking lion in a book! But deep down I was beginning to see he was a lot more than that.

The plane was quite crowded by the time we got on. Kate and I managed to get seats together, but Billy and Adrian had to split up.

"I've hardly had a chance to talk to you all day," Kate said, after the plane had taken off and she was breathing normally again. "I'm so sorry we weren't able to bring Caroline back with us like we'd hoped. You must be really gutted."

"It's OK," I surprised myself by replying. "She's happy there and I'm going to see her again in a couple of weeks." I told her what Adrian had said about God not being like a magician.

Kate thought for a moment. "That's true, I suppose, but it's good to know God does often answer our prayers the way we want him to, even if we have to wait for a while."

"Like when?" I asked.

"Like now. Look at my dad over there. This time two days ago he hadn't left the house in months and now he's thousands of feet up in the air. And…" She stopped and looked at me.

"And what?" I demanded.

"Well, there's you. For ages I've been praying you'll want to know more about God and now you do."

"Do I?"

Kate smiled and picked up her magazine.

I leaned back in my seat and stared out the plane window into the darkness. Kate was right. I didn't feel angry with God anymore as I was starting to realise he did care about me after all. I had a mum and dad who both loved me, though they weren't together, and now I had two sets of grandparents. I glanced over at Kate, who was flicking through some pop star pin-ups.

Not to mention a certain aunt, who was the best mate a guy could ever have.

So, you've finished the book!

Where would you like to go next?

Follow the arrows and then look up the page numbers to find all the details.

Are you like Jack? Would you like to find out more about prayer?

Maybe later

Yes

Massive Prayer Adventure
All you ever wanted to know about prayer, and much more in this great scrapbook! A whole load of fun in 128 pages! See page 110.

Fancy another story? Want something similar to *Jack and the Wardrobe*?

Are you a boy? Head this way…

Are you a girl? Dance down here…

Give **Flexible Kid** a try! Cassie loves her friends, but does a new face in her class mean a new friend, or goodbye to all her old ones? Look at page 110.

Try **Mista Rymz**!
Wes has got trouble: his cousin Jake. And he has to share his room with him. What could be worse? Check out page 110.

Something else? Want to escape to a different world?

Dare you wander down **The Dangerous Road**? Gwilym is on his first trip as a shepherd through the dangerous roads of Wales, but he doesn't realise how dangerous this first trip will be. Wander to page 111.

Open **The Book of Secrets**! Jamie and Rob live in Scotland, but it's not like you know it. The sea has taken over and when they find a book in a seal-skin bag, their adventures start... to threaten their lives! Sail to page 111.

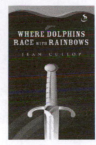

Find out exactly **Where Dolphins Race with Rainbows**! Luke and Rosie sail into a storm, but when they come out the other side, they're in a different country. A country where battles, revolutions and capture awaits! Race to page 111.

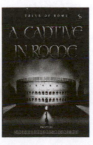

What's it like to be **A Captive in Rome**? Bryn is a Briton, but when his tribe is defeated by the Romans, he is taken prisoner and sold as a slave in Rome! Escape to page 111.

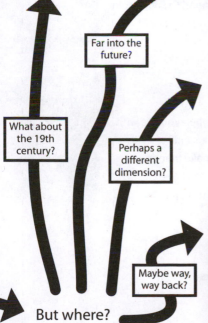

Far into the future?

What about the 19th century?

Perhaps a different dimension?

Maybe way, way back?

But where?

So, you've finished the book!

Check out these great books from Scripture Union! Look at page 112 for details of how to get hold of them.

Massive Prayer Adventure

Sarah Mayers

How you talk and listen to God will be different from anyone else. Discover your personal prayer style with puzzles and quizzes. Try out new places and ideas for meeting God on your own or with your mates. Pray inside and outside, draw, txt and even fly prayers to God!

£4.99, 978 184427 211 2

Mista Rymz

Ruth Kirtley

Wes always thought of himself as a nice guy, but when his cousin Jake comes to stay, his patience is tested to the limit. Jake is the most annoying person on the planet! Can Wes hold it together or will Jake the Snake make him sssssssssnap?!

£3.99, 978 184427 163 4

Flexible Kid

Kay Kinnear

Cassie's life is all about being flexible. Well, when you live with your gran and your dad works on a ship thousands of miles away, it has to be. But when Cassie tries to make friends with Leyla, an asylum seeker from a place Cassie can't even pronounce, her flexible life looks like it might snap in two.

£4.99, 978 184427 165 8

The Dangerous Road

Eleanor Watkins

Gwilym and his dog are on their first trip taking his father's sheep to market. They'd be having a good time if Huw, the old shepherd, didn't always spoil their fun. But soon the dangers of the journey threaten to put a stop to their fun, and their lives.

£4.99, 978 184427 302 7

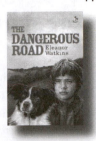

The Book of Secrets

Kathy Lee

In the future, the sea has taken over, turning huge mountains into islands and swallowing cities. The Ancestors disappeared, but some humans still struggle on, fishing and hunting. But when Jamie and his friend Rob find a book in a seal-skin bag, their lives change for ever.

£4.99, 978 184427 342 3

Where Dolphins Race with Rainbows

Jean Cullop

Luke opened his eyes. He was sprawled on the sand – the sea was calm and deep blue. Was the terrible storm a dream? But this was not the town of Poldawn, and he was being watched by a group of strange people. What is this land to which the dolphins have brought Luke and Rosie?

£4.99, 978 184427 383 5

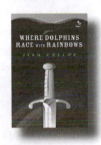

A Captive in Rome

Kathy Lee

"Conan, my brother, looked up the hill, where our dead and dying soldiers lay… hundreds of them, too many to count. In the distance I heard the sound of a Roman trumpet." A disastrous battle tears Brin's world apart. Captured and taken into slavery, he is forced to start a new life in the incredible city of Rome!

£4.99, 978 184427 088 0

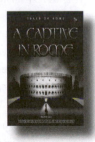

Great books from Scripture Union

Fiction

Mista Rymz, Ruth Kirtley £3.99, 978 184427 163 4
Flexible Kid, Kay Kinnear £4.99, 978 184427 165 8
The Dangerous Road, Eleanor Watkins £4.99, 978 184427 302 7
The Book of Secrets, Kathy Lee £4.99, 978 184427 342 3
Where Dolphins Race with Rainbows, Jean Cullop £4.99, 978 184427 383 5
A Captive in Rome, Kathy Lee £4.99, 978 184427 088 0
Fire By Night, Hannah MacFarlane £4.99, 978 184427 323 2

Fiction by Patricia St John

Rainbow Garden £4.99, 978 184427 300 3
Star of Light £4.99, 978 184427 296 9
The Mystery of Pheasant Cottage £4.99, 978 184427 296 9
The Tanglewoods' Secret £4.99, 978 184427 301 0
Treasures of the Snow £5.99, 978 184427 298 3
Where the River Begins £4.99, 978 184427 299 0

Bible and Prayer

The 10 Must Know Stories, Heather Butler £3.99, 978 184427 326 3
10 Rulz, Andy Bianchi £4.99, 978 184427 053 8
Parabulz, Andy Bianchi £4.99, 978 184427 227 3
Massive Prayer Adventure, Sarah Mayers £4.99, 978 184427 211 2

God and you!

No Girls Allowed, Darren Hill and Alex Taylor £4.99, 978 184427 209 9
Friends Forever, Mary Taylor £4.99, 978 184427 210 5

Puzzle books

Bible Codecrackers: Moses, Valerie Hornsby £3.99, 978 184427 181 8
Bible Codecrackers: Jesus, Gillian Ellis £3.99, 978 184427 207 5
Bible Codecrackers: Peter & Paul, Gillian Ellis £3.99, 978 184427 208 2

Available from your local Christian bookshop or from
Scripture Union Mail Order, PO Box 5148, Milton Keynes MLO, MK2 2YX
Tel: 0845 07 06 006   Website: www.scriptureunion.org.uk/shop
All prices correct at time of going to print.